Robert Louis Stevenson's
THE STRANGE CASE OF

Dr. Jekyll and

Mr. HyDE

CAMPFIRE™

KALYANI NAVYUG MEDIA PVT. LTD
New Delhi

Sitting around the Campfire, telling the story, were:

Wordsmith	:	C. E. L. Welsh
Penciler	:	Lalit Kumar Sharma
Inker	:	Jagdish Kumar
Colorist	:	Vijay Sharma
Letterers	:	Bhavnath Chaudhary
		Laxmi Chand Gupta
Editors	:	Divya Dubey
		Eman Chowdhary
Editor (Informative Content)	:	Pushpanjali Borooah
Production Controller	:	Vishal Sharma

Cover Artists:

Illustrator	:	Lalit Kumar Sharma
Colorist	:	Vijay Sharma
Designer	:	Jayakrishnan K. P.

Published by Kalyani Navyug Media Pvt. Ltd
101 C, Shiv House, Hari Nagar Ashram
New Delhi 110014
India
www.campfire.co.in

ISBN: 978-93-80741-30-7

Printed in India at Tara Art Printers Pvt. Ltd

About the Author

Robert Louis Stevenson was born in Edinburgh, Scotland, in 1850. The son of an engineer, Stevenson followed in his father's footsteps by studying engineering and law at the University of Edinburgh. However, his passion for writing soon became more than a hobby, and he decided to pursue it on a full-time basis. This career choice initially upset his father, but Stevenson made a promise to complete his studies, and was admitted to the Scottish Bar in 1875.

Stevenson's most famous work is the classic pirate tale *Treasure Island*, which was published in 1883. A fast-paced story of adventure with mass appeal, it soon became popular across the world. In the 125 years since then, readers of all ages have delighted in following the exploits of young Jim Hawkins as he travels to a remote island in search of buried gold. Stevenson later created an infamous, but very intriguing character in *The Strange Case of Dr. Jekyll and Mr. Hyde*, published in 1886. His adventure story *Kidnapped*, a tale of a young boy and a stolen inheritance, was also published in the same year.

Throughout his life, Stevenson was frequently in poor health, and he often traveled abroad in search of places with mild climates. He also wrote a number of essays detailing these trips. During one such journey to France, he met an American woman named Frances Osbourne, and later married her during a visit to California.

In 1887, Stevenson headed for America with his wife, stepson, and mother. He had become famous in New York, and received many attractive offers from various publishers. It was soon after this move that he took up his pen for *The Master of Ballantrae*, a novel which is considered one of his best works.

Stevenson eventually settled with his family on the island of Samoa, where he died at the age of 44 on December 3, 1894. While best known for writing tales of action and adventure, Robert Louis Stevenson is also remembered as an accomplished poet and essayist.

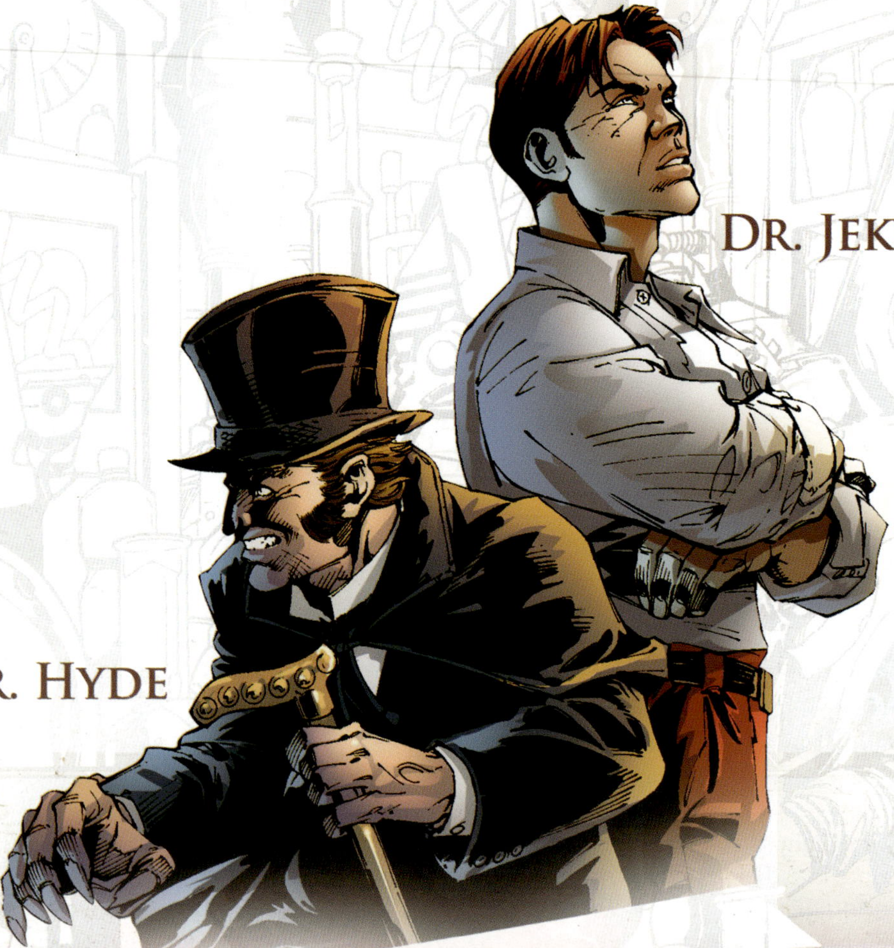

DR. JEKYLL

MR. HYDE

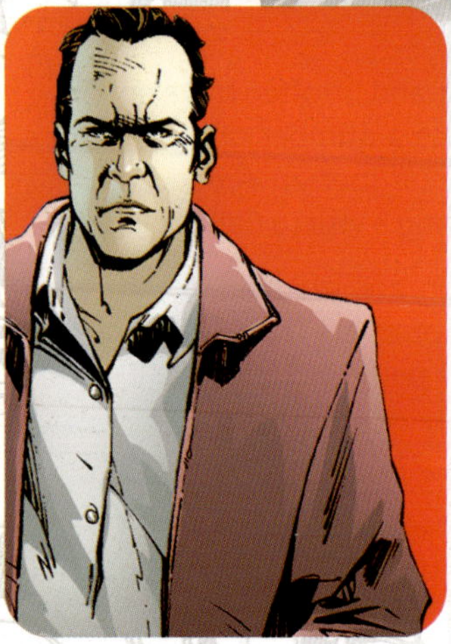

UTTERSON

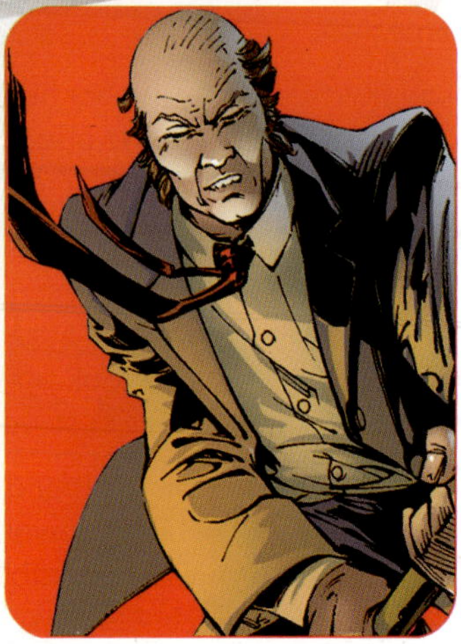

POOLE

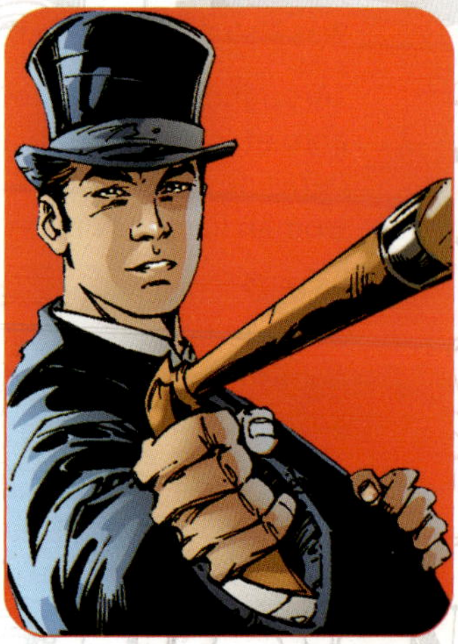

ENFIELD

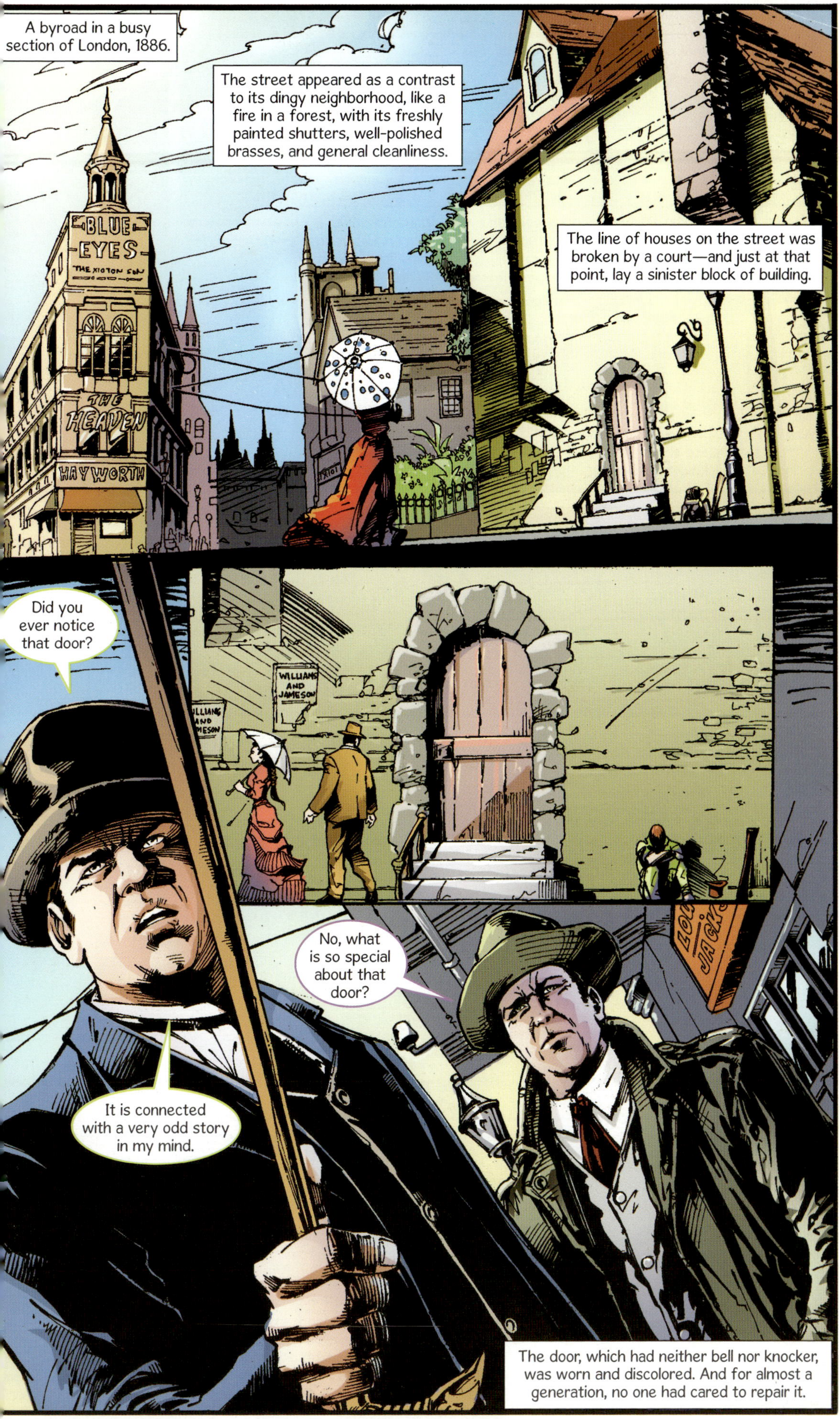
A byroad in a busy section of London, 1886.
The street appeared as a contrast to its dingy neighborhood, like a fire in a forest, with its freshly painted shutters, well-polished brasses, and general cleanliness.
BLUE EYES
THE HEAVEN
HAYWORTH
The line of houses on the street was broken by a court—and just at that point, lay a sinister block of building.
Did you ever notice that door?
WILLIAMS AND JAMESON
No, what is so special about that door?
It is connected with a very odd story in my mind.
The door, which had neither bell nor knocker, was worn and discolored. And for almost a generation, no one had cared to repair it.

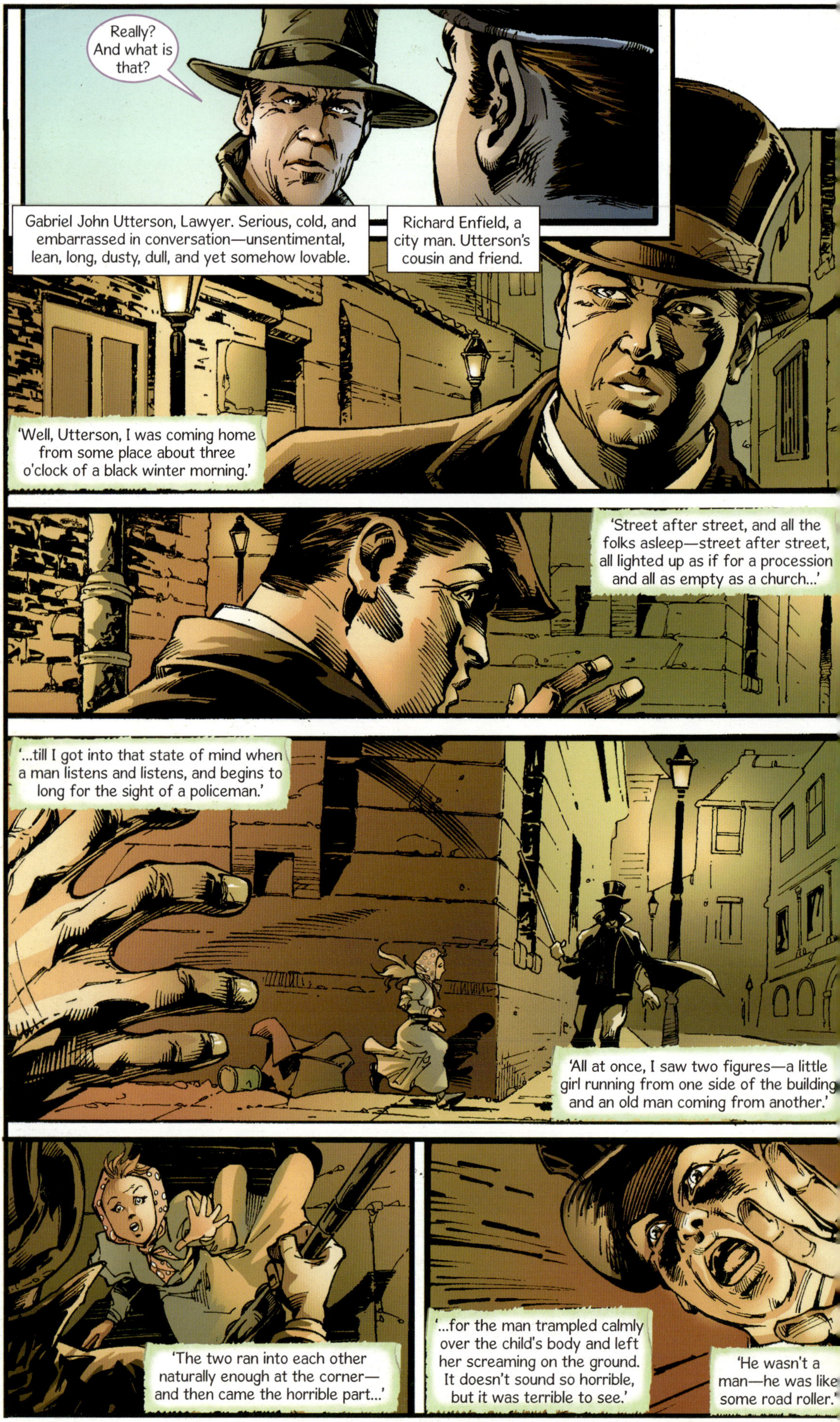

Really? And what is that?
Gabriel John Utterson, Lawyer. Serious, cold, and embarrassed in conversation—unsentimental, lean, long, dusty, dull, and yet somehow lovable.
Richard Enfield, a city man. Utterson's cousin and friend.
'Well, Utterson, I was coming home from some place about three o'clock of a black winter morning.'
'Street after street, and all the folks asleep—street after street, all lighted up as if for a procession and all as empty as a church...'
'...till I got into that state of mind when a man listens and listens, and begins to long for the sight of a policeman.'
'All at once, I saw two figures—a little girl running from one side of the building and an old man coming from another.'
'The two ran into each other naturally enough at the corner—and then came the horrible part...'
'...for the man trampled calmly over the child's body and left her screaming on the ground. It doesn't sound so horrible, but it was terrible to see.'
'He wasn't a man—he was like some road roller.'

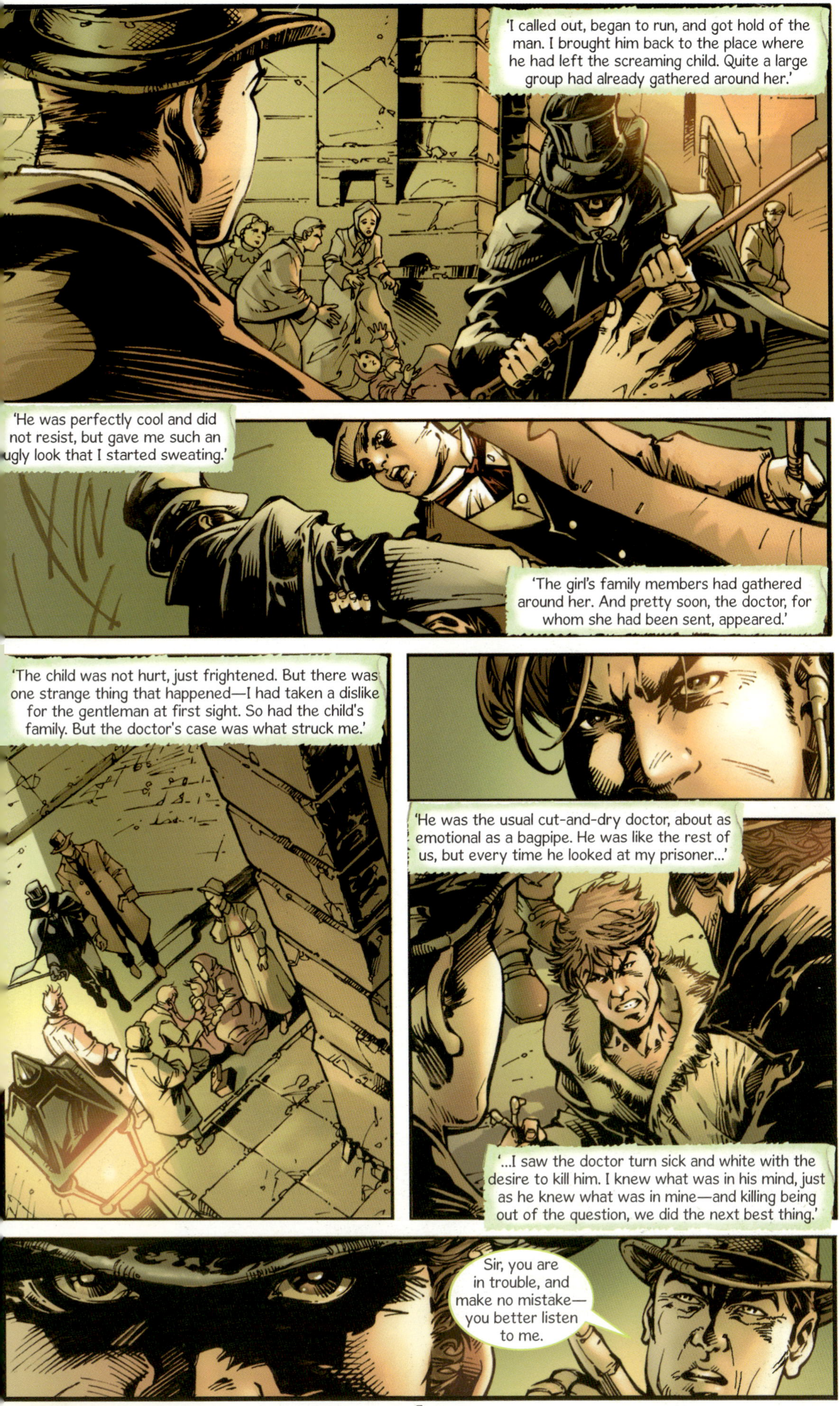
'I called out, began to run, and got hold of the man. I brought him back to the place where he had left the screaming child. Quite a large group had already gathered around her.'
'He was perfectly cool and did not resist, but gave me such an ugly look that I started sweating.'
'The girl's family members had gathered around her. And pretty soon, the doctor, for whom she had been sent, appeared.'
'The child was not hurt, just frightened. But there was one strange thing that happened—I had taken a dislike for the gentleman at first sight. So had the child's family. But the doctor's case was what struck me.'
'He was the usual cut-and-dry doctor, about as emotional as a bagpipe. He was like the rest of us, but every time he looked at my prisoner...'
'...I saw the doctor turn sick and white with the desire to kill him. I knew what was in his mind, just as he knew what was in mine—and killing being out of the question, we did the next best thing.'
Sir, you are in trouble, and make no mistake—you better listen to me.

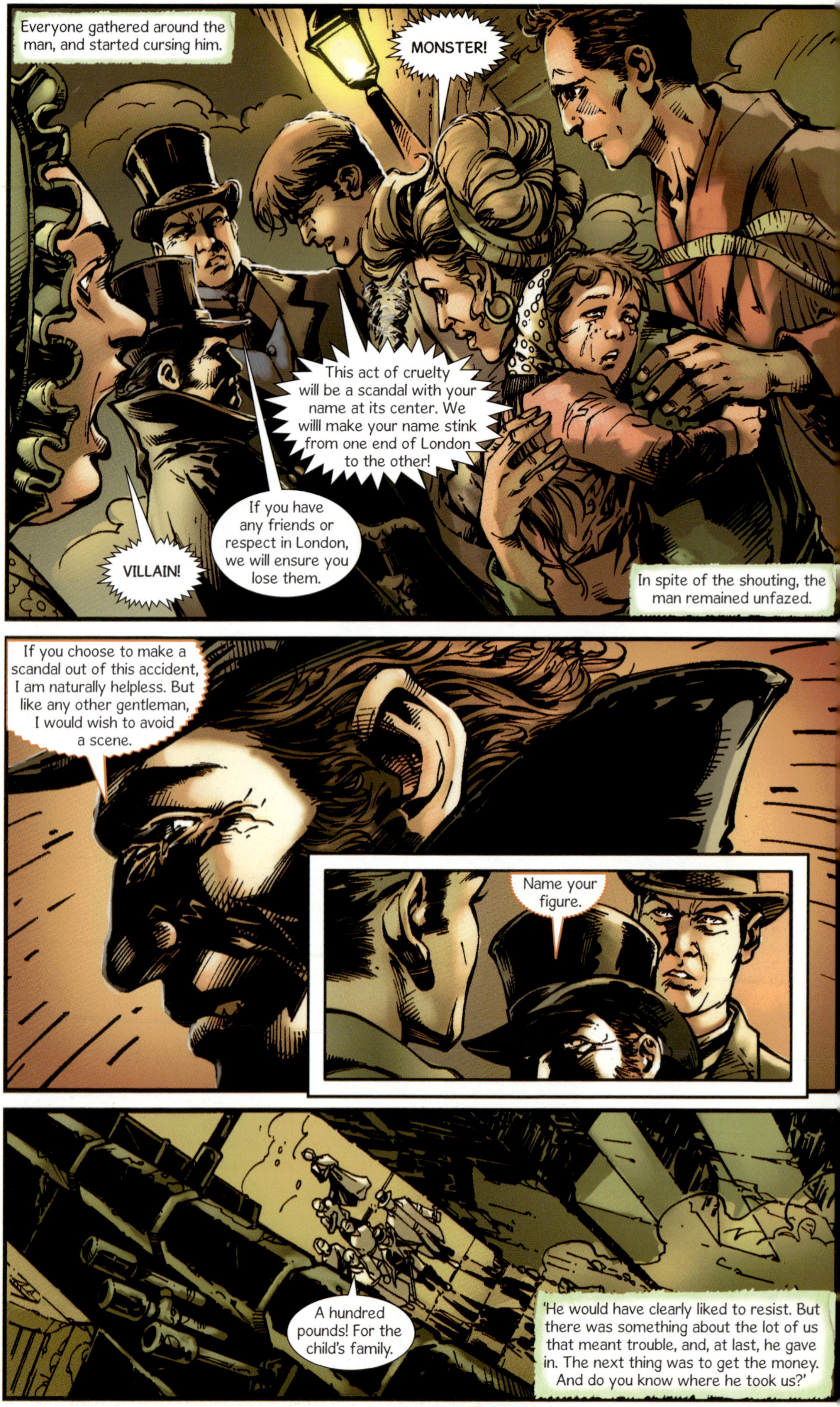
Everyone gathered around the man, and started cursing him.
MONSTER!
This act of cruelty will be a scandal with your name at its center. We willl make your name stink from one end of London to the other!
If you have any friends or respect in London, we will ensure you lose them.
VILLAIN!
In spite of the shouting, the man remained unfazed.
If you choose to make a scandal out of this accident, I am naturally helpless. But like any other gentleman, I would wish to avoid a scene.
Name your figure.
A hundred pounds! For the child's family.
'He would have clearly liked to resist. But there was something about the lot of us that meant trouble, and, at last, he gave in. The next thing was to get the money. And do you know where he took us?'

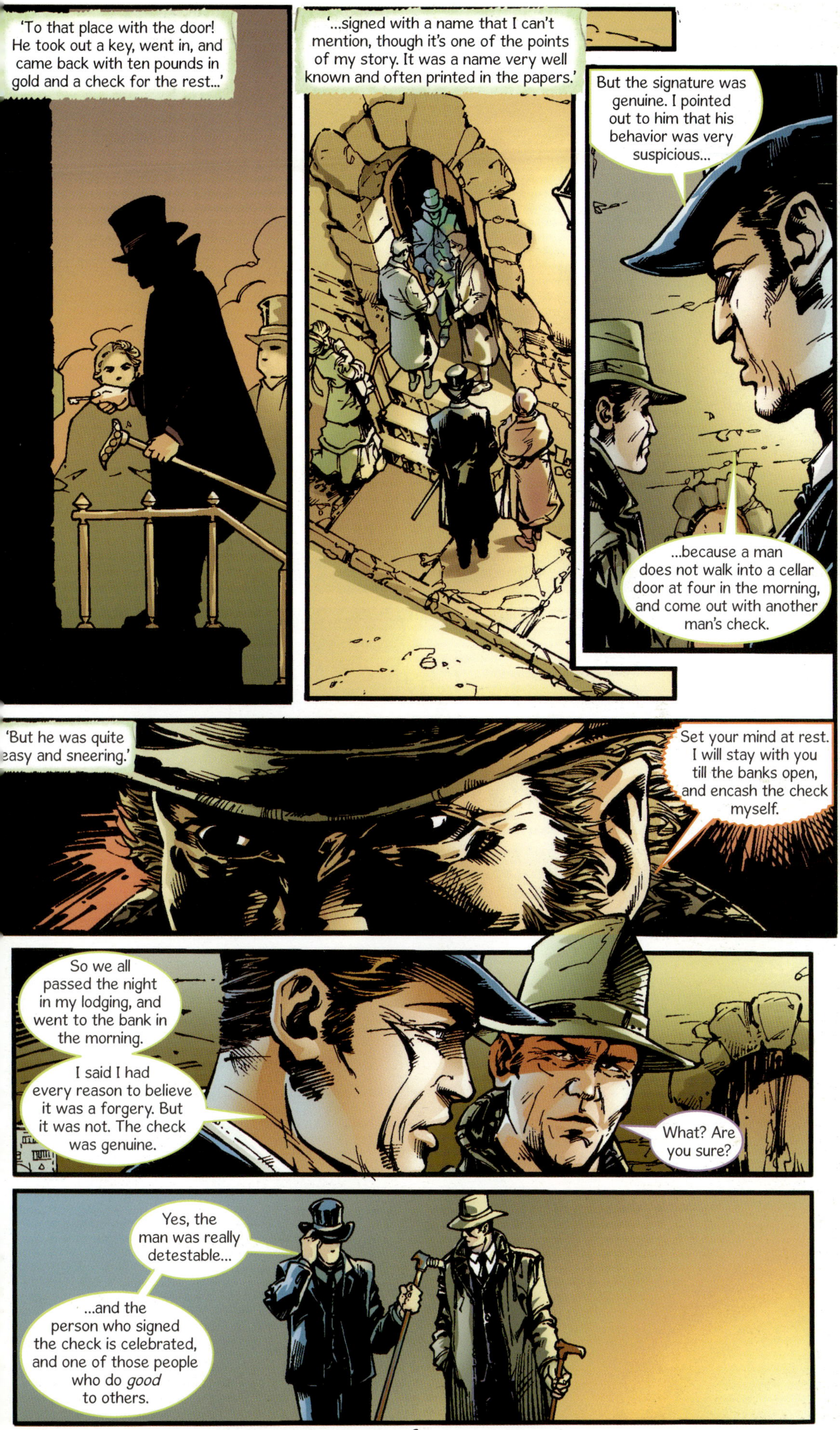
'To that place with the door! He took out a key, went in, and came back with ten pounds in gold and a check for the rest...'
'...signed with a name that I can't mention, though it's one of the points of my story. It was a name very well known and often printed in the papers.'
But the signature was genuine. I pointed out to him that his behavior was very suspicious...
...because a man does not walk into a cellar door at four in the morning, and come out with another man's check.
'But he was quite easy and sneering.'
Set your mind at rest. I will stay with you till the banks open, and encash the check myself.
So we all passed the night in my lodging, and went to the bank in the morning.
I said I had every reason to believe it was a forgery. But it was not. The check was genuine.
What? Are you sure?
Yes, the man was really detestable...
...and the person who signed the check is celebrated, and one of those people who do *good* to others.

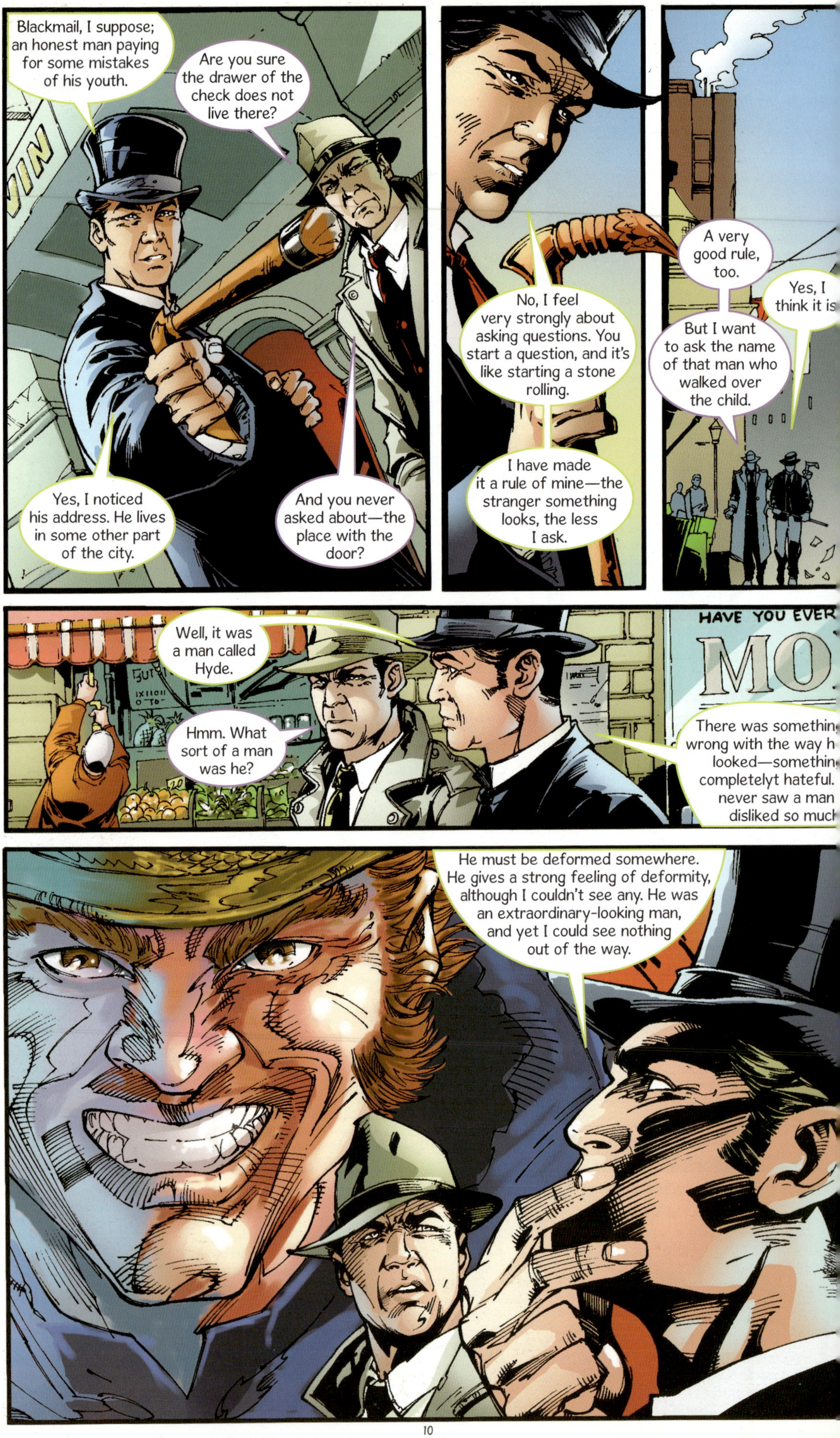
Blackmail, I suppose; an honest man paying for some mistakes of his youth.
Are you sure the drawer of the check does not live there?
Yes, I noticed his address. He lives in some other part of the city.
And you never asked about—the place with the door?
No, I feel very strongly about asking questions. You start a question, and it's like starting a stone rolling.
I have made it a rule of mine—the stranger something looks, the less I ask.
A very good rule, too.
Yes, I think it is
But I want to ask the name of that man who walked over the child.
Well, it was a man called Hyde.
Hmm. What sort of a man was he?
HAVE YOU EVER
MO
There was somethin wrong with the way h looked—somethin completelyt hateful. never saw a man disliked so much
He must be deformed somewhere. He gives a strong feeling of deformity, although I couldn't see any. He was an extraordinary-looking man, and yet I could see nothing out of the way.

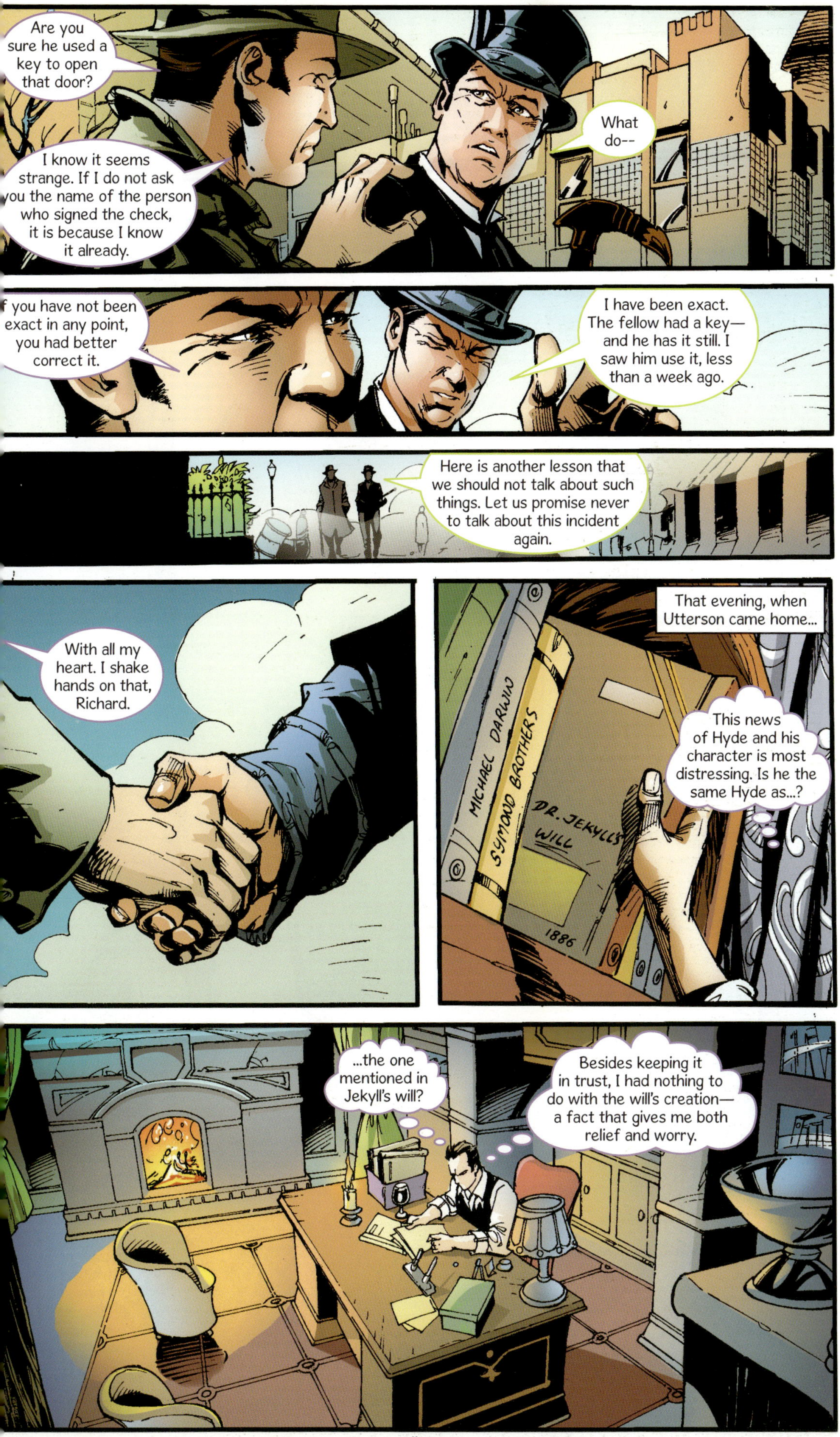
Are you sure he used a key to open that door?
I know it seems strange. If I do not ask you the name of the person who signed the check, it is because I know it already.
What do--
If you have not been exact in any point, you had better correct it.
I have been exact. The fellow had a key—and he has it still. I saw him use it, less than a week ago.
Here is another lesson that we should not talk about such things. Let us promise never to talk about this incident again.
With all my heart. I shake hands on that, Richard.
That evening, when Utterson came home...
MICHAEL DARWIN
SYMOND BROTHERS
DR. JEKYLL'S WILL
1886
This news of Hyde and his character is most distressing. Is he the same Hyde as...?
...the one mentioned in Jekyll's will?
Besides keeping it in trust, I had nothing to do with the will's creation—a fact that gives me both relief and worry.

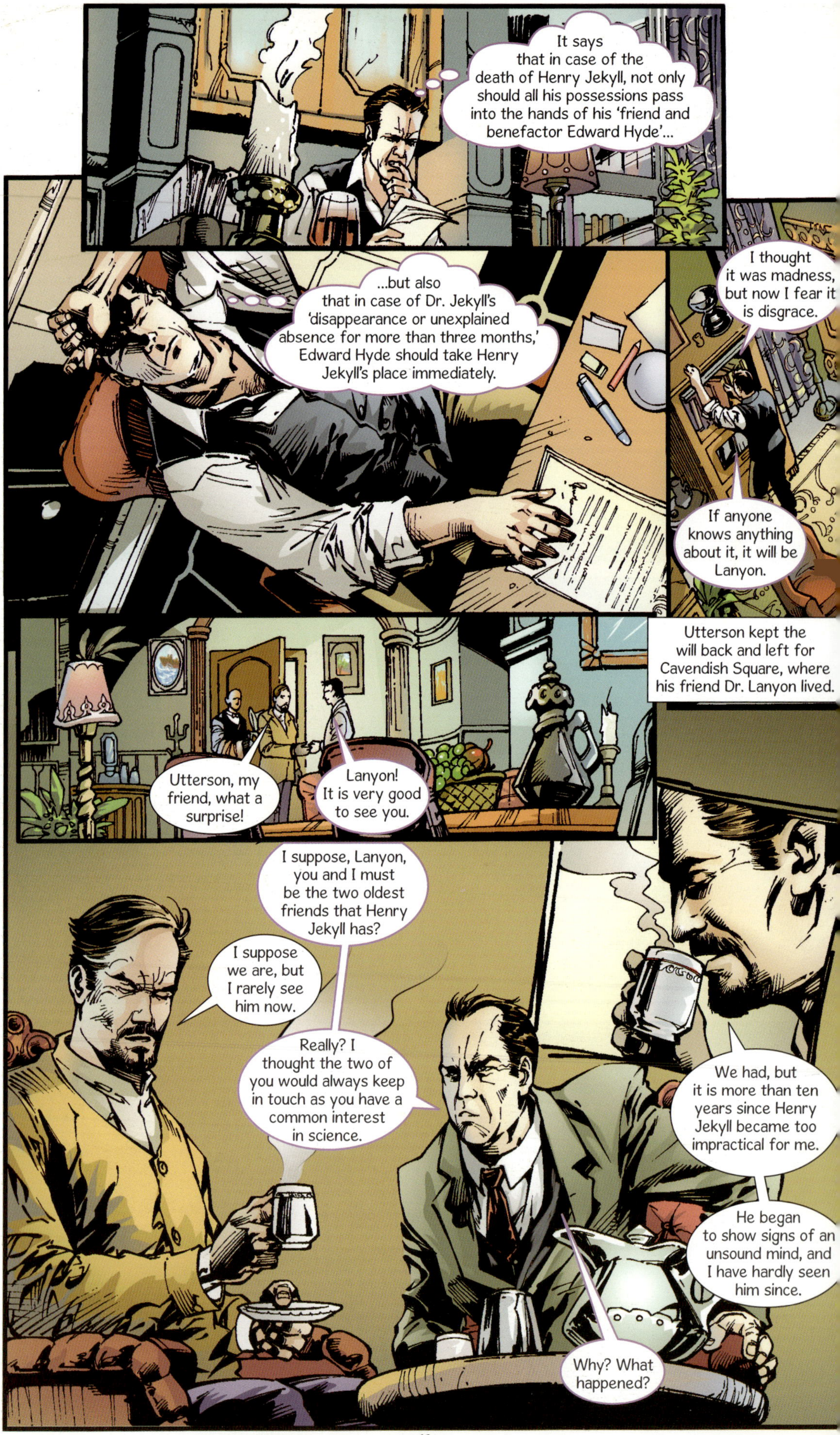
It says that in case of the death of Henry Jekyll, not only should all his possessions pass into the hands of his 'friend and benefactor Edward Hyde'...
...but also that in case of Dr. Jekyll's 'disappearance or unexplained absence for more than three months,' Edward Hyde should take Henry Jekyll's place immediately.
I thought it was madness, but now I fear it is disgrace.
If anyone knows anything about it, it will be Lanyon.
Utterson kept the will back and left for Cavendish Square, where his friend Dr. Lanyon lived.
Utterson, my friend, what a surprise!
Lanyon! It is very good to see you.
I suppose, Lanyon, you and I must be the two oldest friends that Henry Jekyll has?
I suppose we are, but I rarely see him now.
Really? I thought the two of you would always keep in touch as you have a common interest in science.
We had, but it is more than ten years since Henry Jekyll became too impractical for me.
He began to show signs of an unsound mind, and I have hardly seen him since.
Why? What happened?

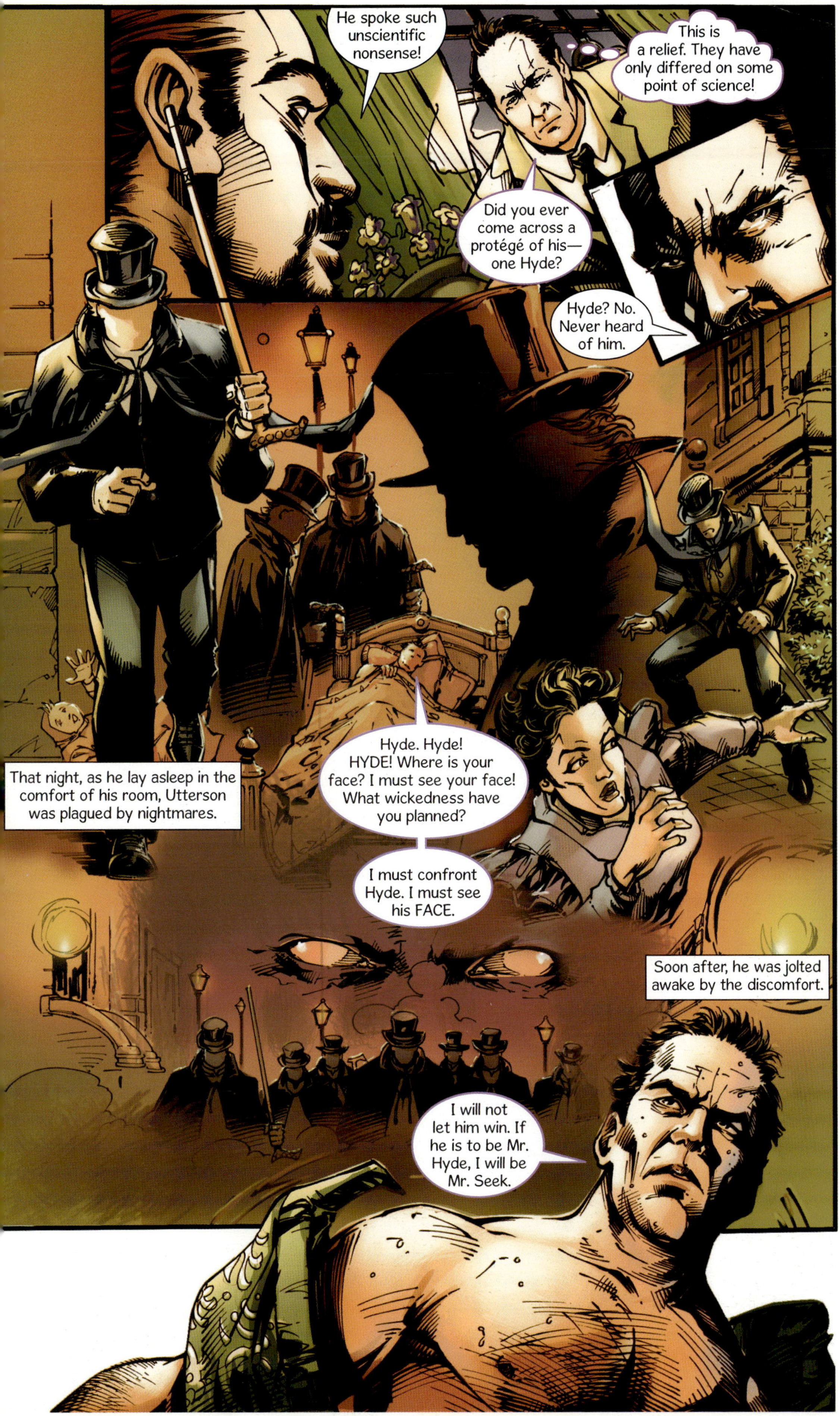
He spoke such unscientific nonsense!
This is a relief. They have only differed on some point of science!
Did you ever come across a protégé of his—one Hyde?
Hyde? No. Never heard of him.
That night, as he lay asleep in the comfort of his room, Utterson was plagued by nightmares.
Hyde. Hyde! HYDE! Where is your face? I must see your face! What wickedness have you planned?
I must confront Hyde. I must see his FACE.
Soon after, he was jolted awake by the discomfort.
I will not let him win. If he is to be Mr. Hyde, I will be Mr. Seek.

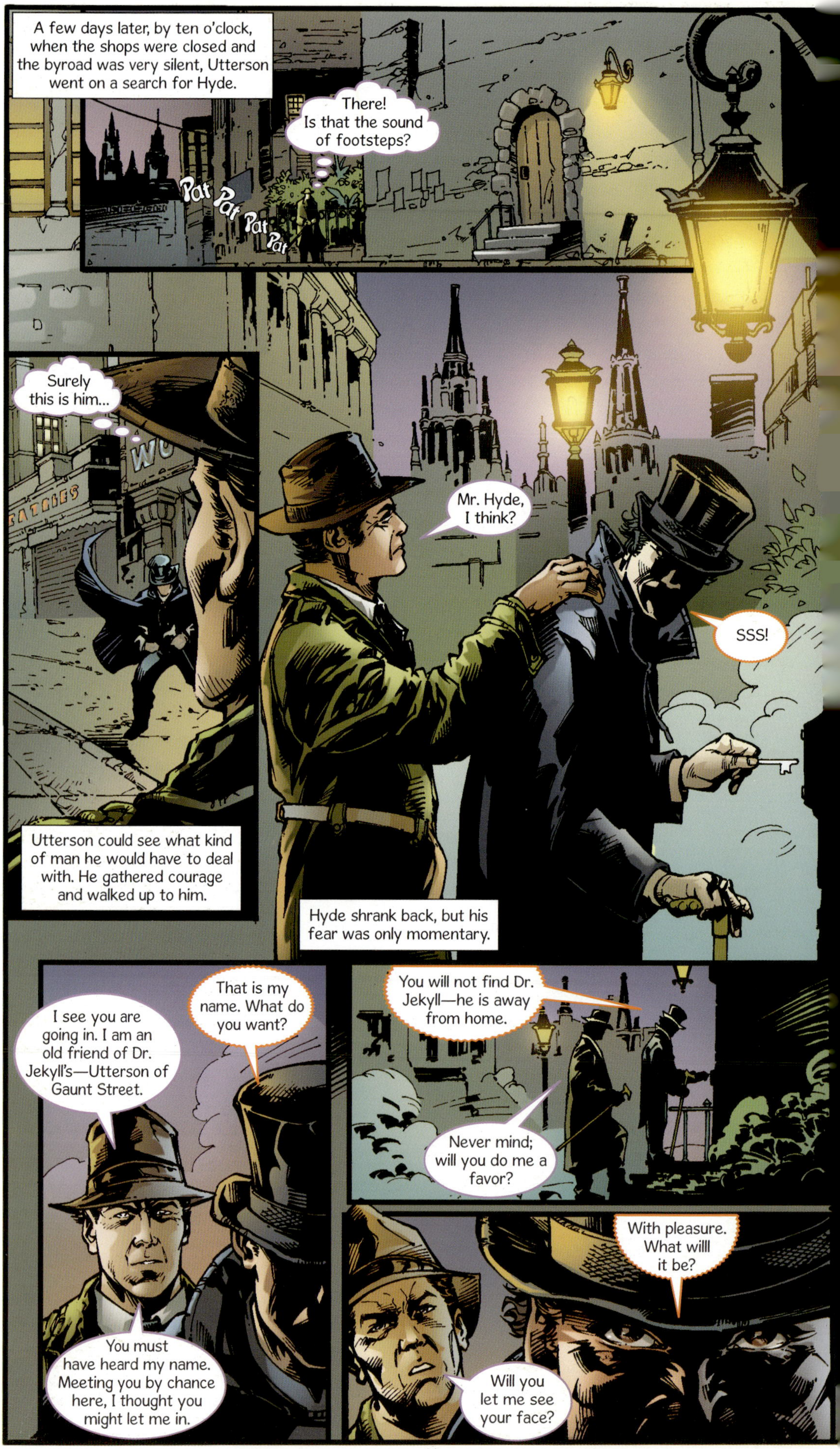
A few days later, by ten o'clock, when the shops were closed and the byroad was very silent, Utterson went on a search for Hyde.
There! Is that the sound of footsteps?
Pat Pat Pat Pat
Surely this is him...
Utterson could see what kind of man he would have to deal with. He gathered courage and walked up to him.
Mr. Hyde, I think?
SSS!
Hyde shrank back, but his fear was only momentary.
I see you are going in. I am an old friend of Dr. Jekyll's—Utterson of Gaunt Street.
That is my name. What do you want?
You must have heard my name. Meeting you by chance here, I thought you might let me in.
You will not find Dr. Jekyll—he is away from home.
Never mind; will you do me a favor?
With pleasure. What willl it be?
Will you let me see your face?

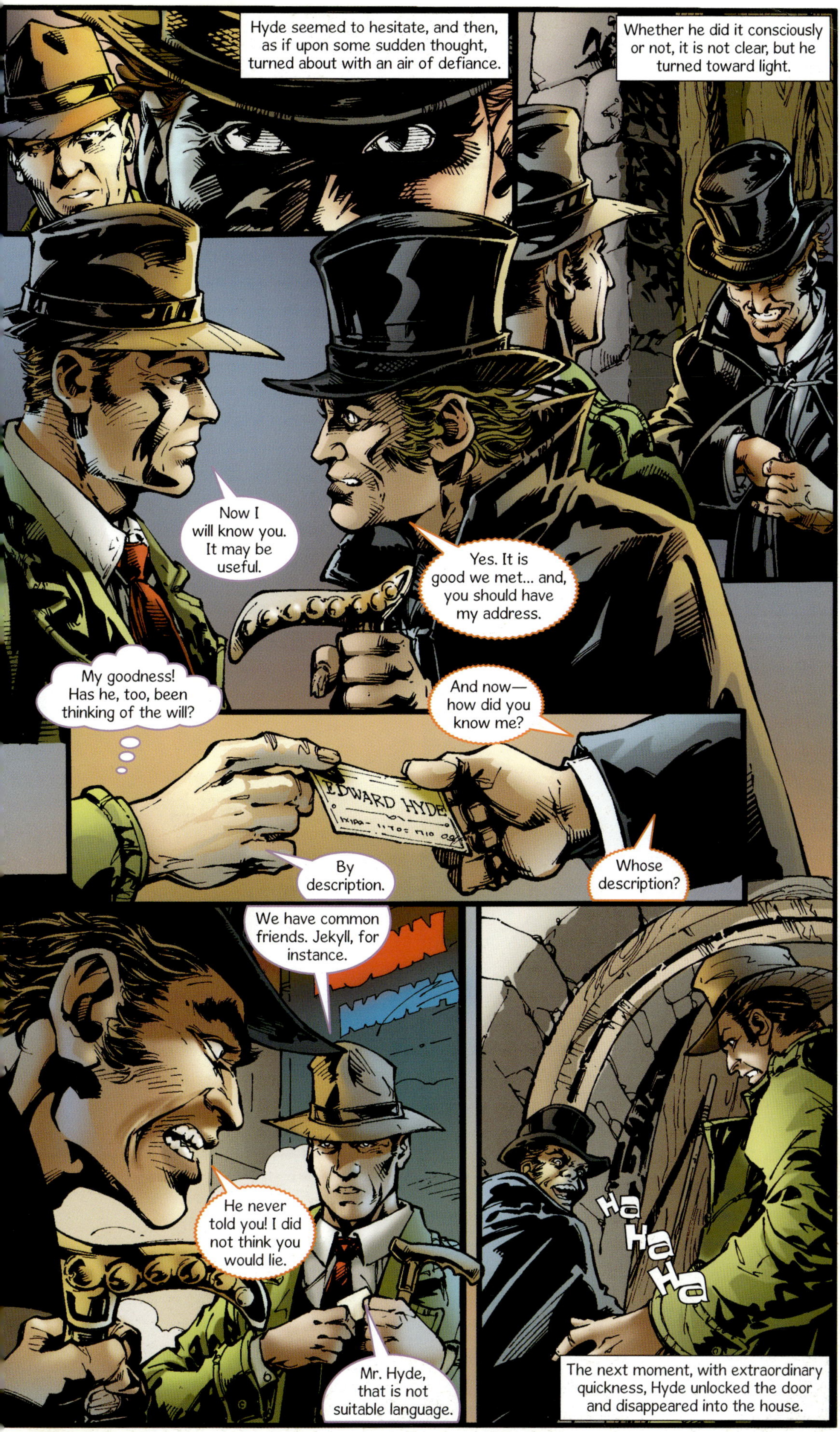

Hyde seemed to hesitate, and then, as if upon some sudden thought, turned about with an air of defiance.
Whether he did it consciously or not, it is not clear, but he turned toward light.
Now I will know you. It may be useful.
Yes. It is good we met... and, you should have my address.
My goodness! Has he, too, been thinking of the will?
And now— how did you know me?
EDWARD HYDE
By description.
Whose description?
We have common friends. Jekyll, for instance.
He never told you! I did not think you would lie.
Mr. Hyde, that is not suitable language.
HA HA HA HA
The next moment, with extraordinary quickness, Hyde unlocked the door and disappeared into the house.

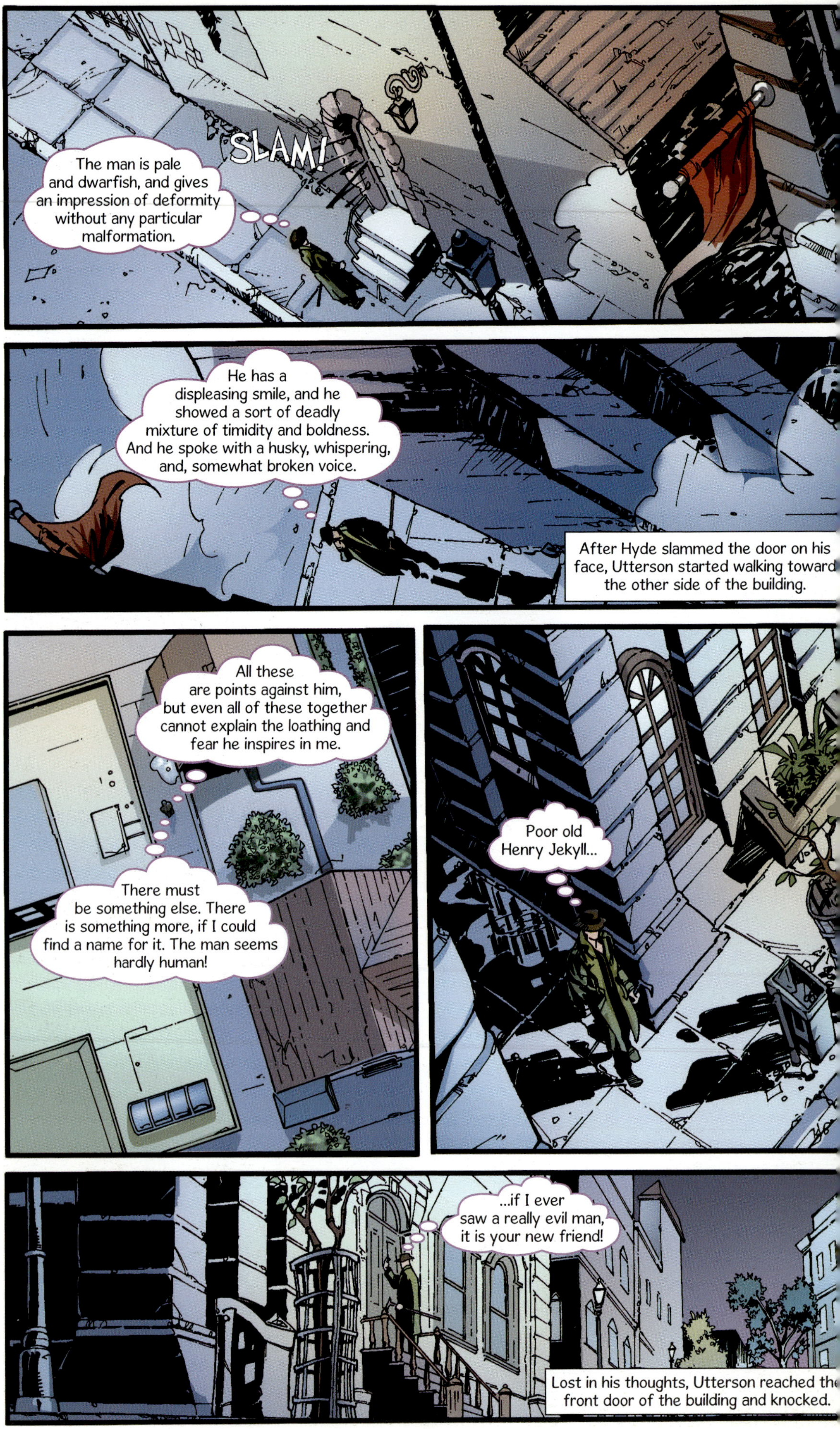
SLAM!
The man is pale and dwarfish, and gives an impression of deformity without any particular malformation.
He has a displeasing smile, and he showed a sort of deadly mixture of timidity and boldness. And he spoke with a husky, whispering, and, somewhat broken voice.
After Hyde slammed the door on his face, Utterson started walking toward the other side of the building.
All these are points against him, but even all of these together cannot explain the loathing and fear he inspires in me.
There must be something else. There is something more, if I could find a name for it. The man seems hardly human!
Poor old Henry Jekyll...
...if I ever saw a really evil man, it is your new friend!
Lost in his thoughts, Utterson reached the front door of the building and knocked.

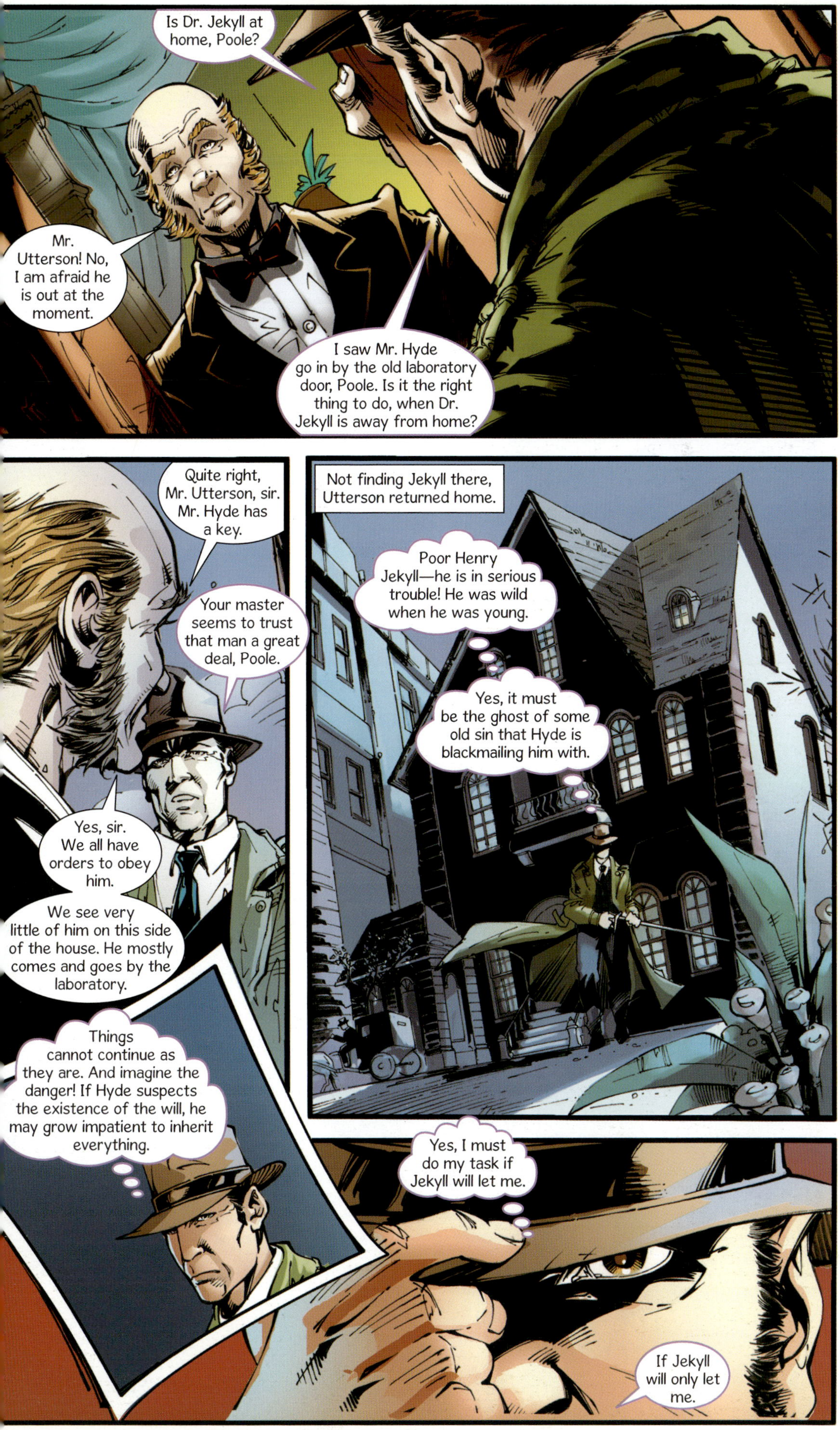

Is Dr. Jekyll at home, Poole?
Mr. Utterson! No, I am afraid he is out at the moment.
I saw Mr. Hyde go in by the old laboratory door, Poole. Is it the right thing to do, when Dr. Jekyll is away from home?
Quite right, Mr. Utterson, sir. Mr. Hyde has a key.
Your master seems to trust that man a great deal, Poole.
Yes, sir. We all have orders to obey him.
We see very little of him on this side of the house. He mostly comes and goes by the laboratory.
Things cannot continue as they are. And imagine the danger! If Hyde suspects the existence of the will, he may grow impatient to inherit everything.
Not finding Jekyll there, Utterson returned home.
Poor Henry Jekyll—he is in serious trouble! He was wild when he was young.
Yes, it must be the ghost of some old sin that Hyde is blackmailing him with.
Yes, I must do my task if Jekyll will let me.
If Jekyll will only let me.

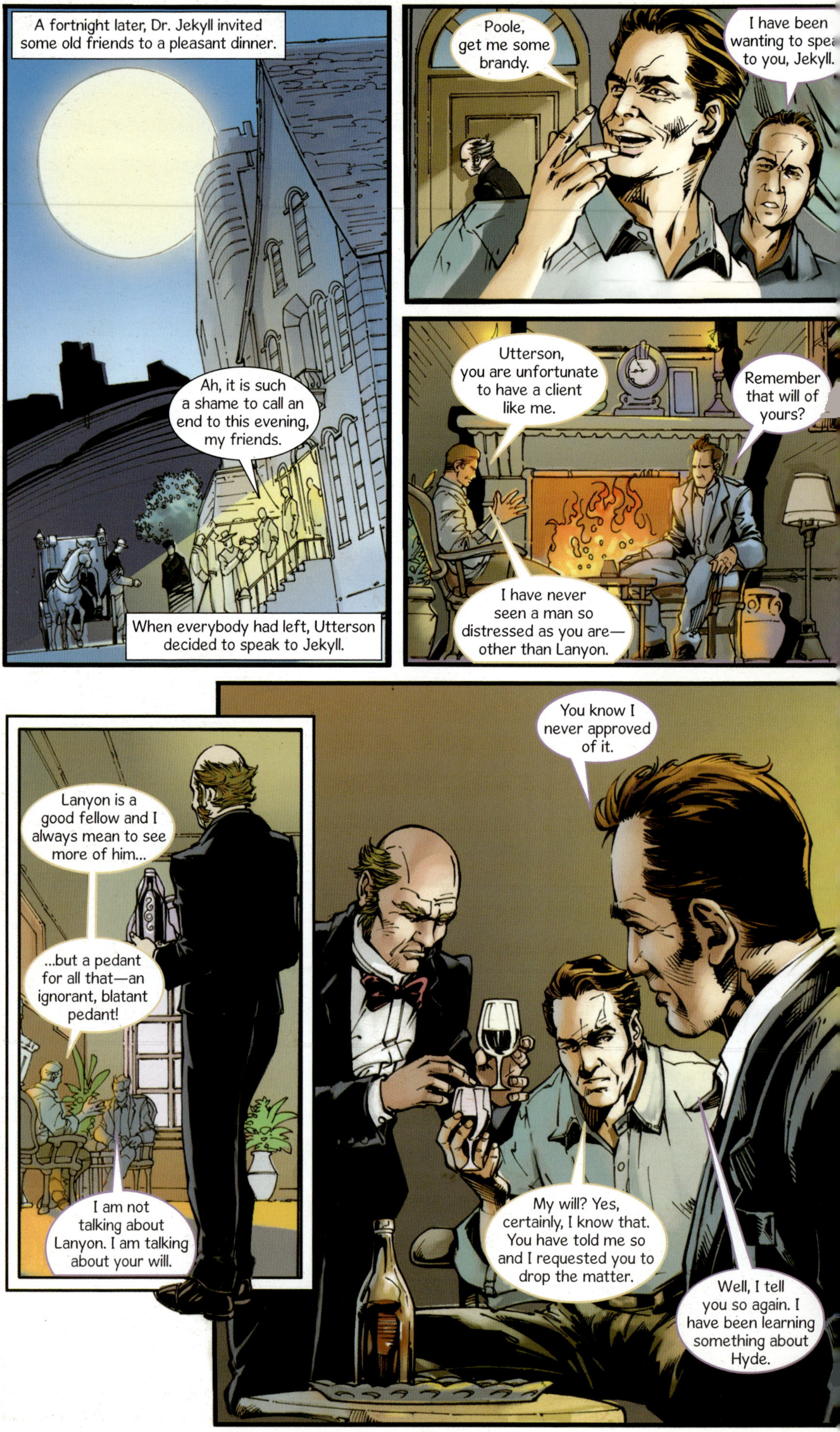

A fortnight later, Dr. Jekyll invited some old friends to a pleasant dinner.
Ah, it is such a shame to call an end to this evening, my friends.
When everybody had left, Utterson decided to speak to Jekyll.
Poole, get me some brandy.
I have been wanting to spea to you, Jekyll.
Utterson, you are unfortunate to have a client like me.
Remember that will of yours?
I have never seen a man so distressed as you are—other than Lanyon.
Lanyon is a good fellow and I always mean to see more of him...
...but a pedant for all that—an ignorant, blatant pedant!
I am not talking about Lanyon. I am talking about your will.
You know I never approved of it.
My will? Yes, certainly, I know that. You have told me so and I requested you to drop the matter.
Well, I tell you so again. I have been learning something about Hyde.

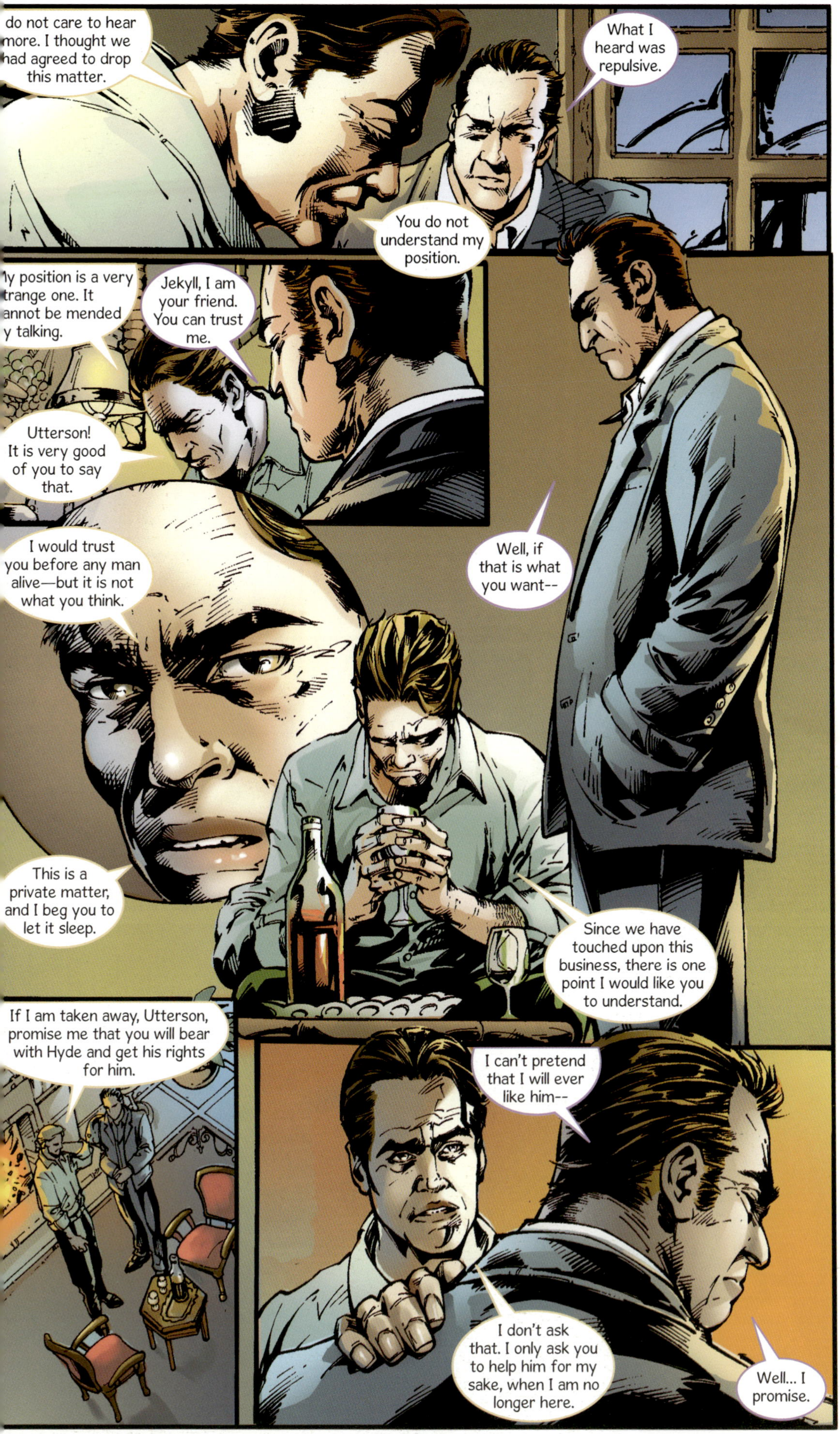

do not care to hear more. I thought we had agreed to drop this matter.
What I heard was repulsive.
You do not understand my position.
ly position is a very trange one. It annot be mended y talking.
Jekyll, I am your friend. You can trust me.
Utterson! It is very good of you to say that.
I would trust you before any man alive—but it is not what you think.
Well, if that is what you want--
This is a private matter, and I beg you to let it sleep.
Since we have touched upon this business, there is one point I would like you to understand.
If I am taken away, Utterson, promise me that you will bear with Hyde and get his rights for him.
I can't pretend that I will ever like him--
I don't ask that. I only ask you to help him for my sake, when I am no longer here.
Well... I promise.

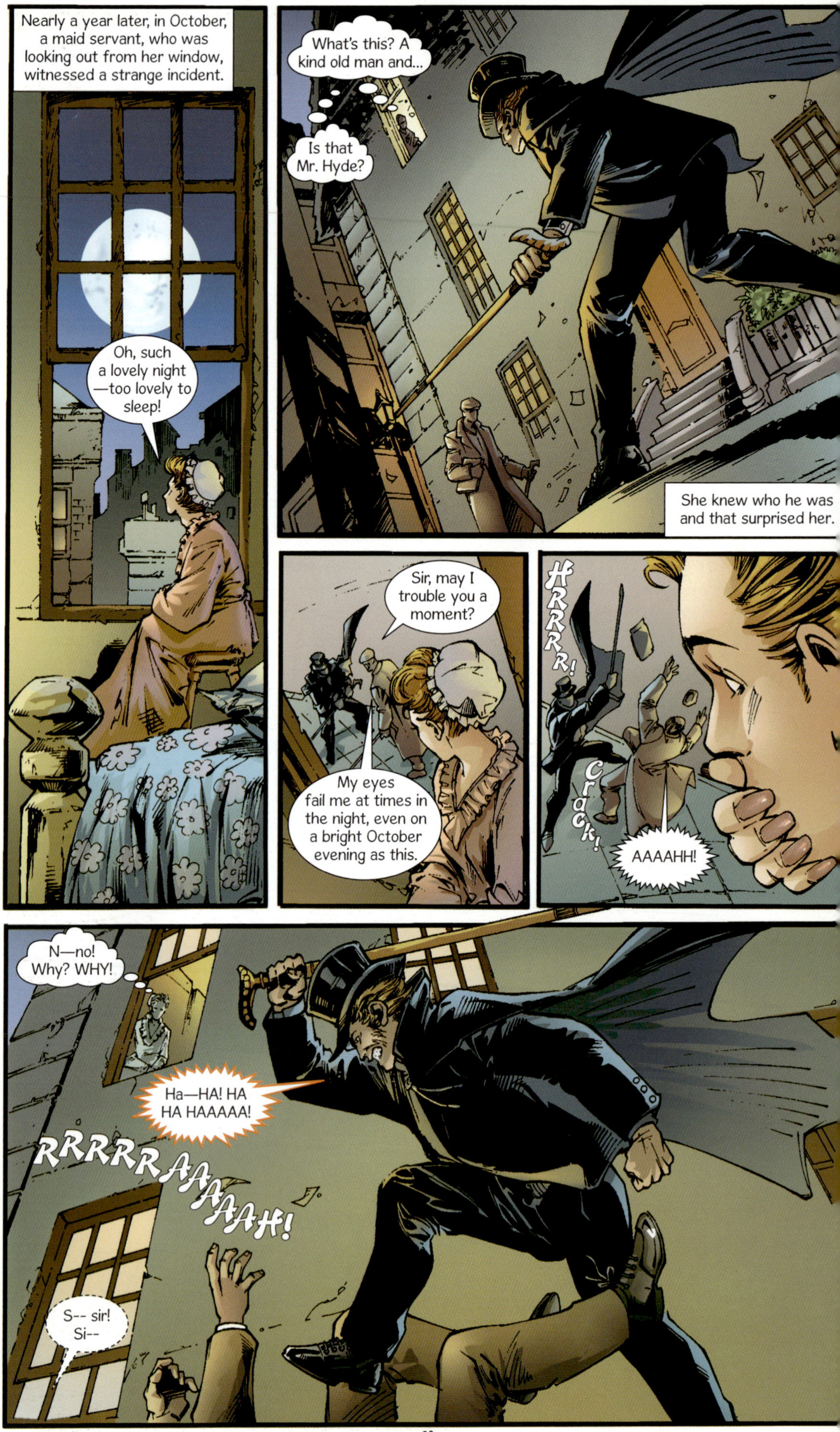

Nearly a year later, in October, a maid servant, who was looking out from her window, witnessed a strange incident.
Oh, such a lovely night—too lovely to sleep!
What's this? A kind old man and...
Is that Mr. Hyde?
She knew who he was and that surprised her.
Sir, may I trouble you a moment?
My eyes fail me at times in the night, even on a bright October evening as this.
HRRRRR!
Crack!
AAAAHH!
N—no! Why? WHY!
Ha—HA! HA HA HAAAAA!
RRRRRRAAAAAAH!
S-- sir! Si--

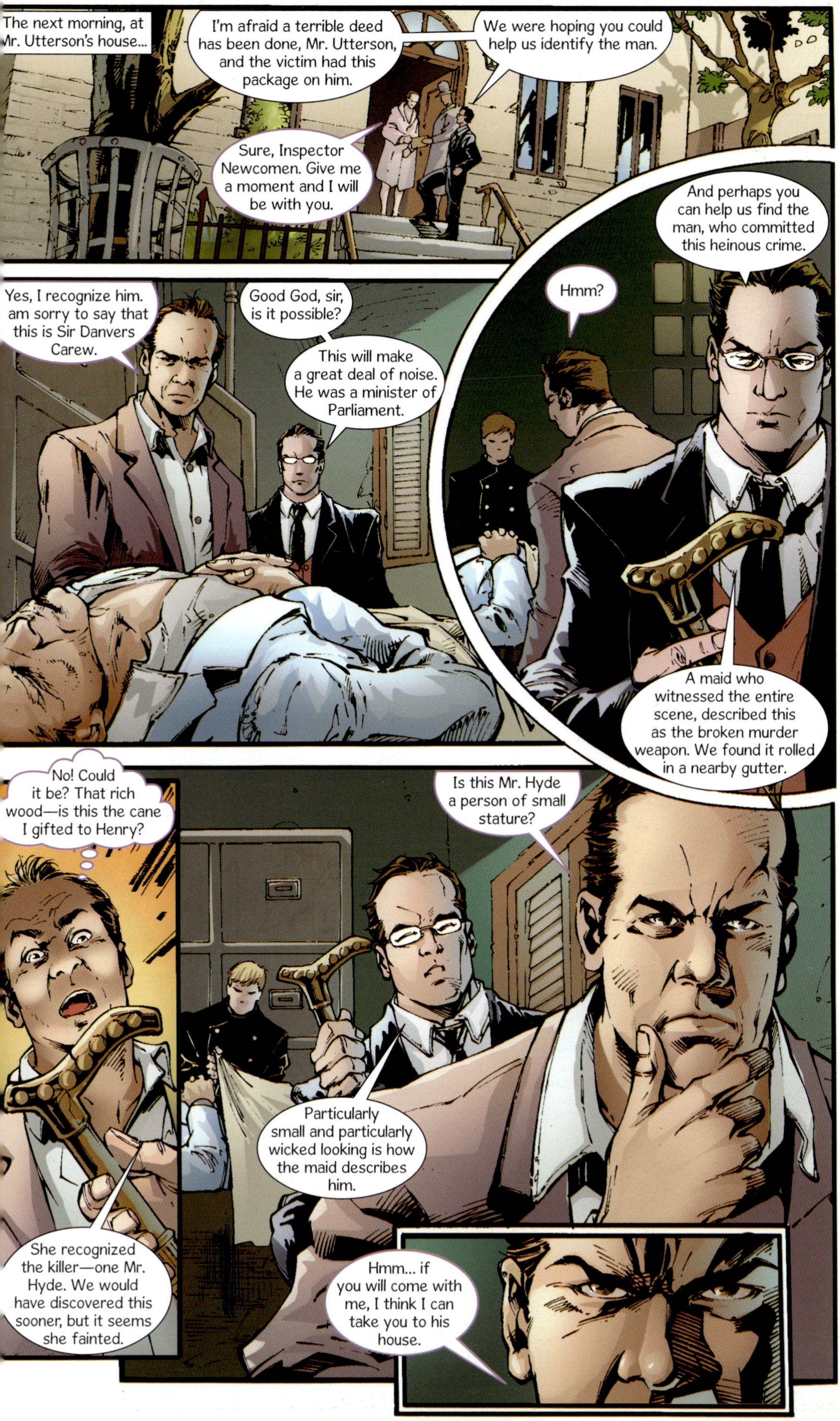
The next morning, at Mr. Utterson's house...
I'm afraid a terrible deed has been done, Mr. Utterson, and the victim had this package on him.
We were hoping you could help us identify the man.
Sure, Inspector Newcomen. Give me a moment and I will be with you.
And perhaps you can help us find the man, who committed this heinous crime.
Yes, I recognize him. I am sorry to say that this is Sir Danvers Carew.
Good God, sir, is it possible?
This will make a great deal of noise. He was a minister of Parliament.
Hmm?
A maid who witnessed the entire scene, described this as the broken murder weapon. We found it rolled in a nearby gutter.
No! Could it be? That rich wood—is this the cane I gifted to Henry?
Is this Mr. Hyde a person of small stature?
Particularly small and particularly wicked looking is how the maid describes him.
She recognized the killer—one Mr. Hyde. We would have discovered this sooner, but it seems she fainted.
Hmm... if you will come with me, I think I can take you to his house.

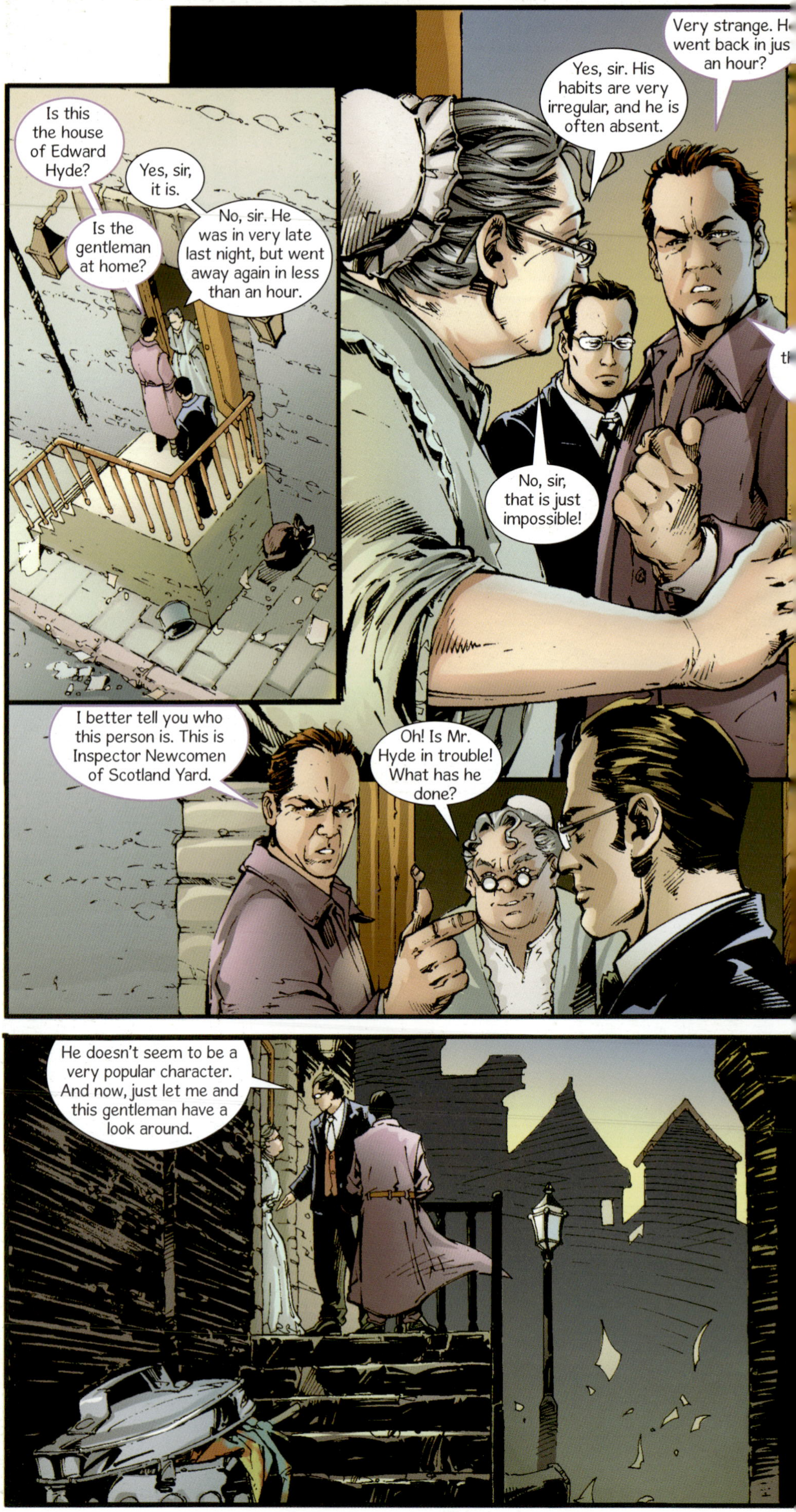
Is this the house of Edward Hyde?
Yes, sir, it is.
Is the gentleman at home?
No, sir. He was in very late last night, but went away again in less than an hour.
Yes, sir. His habits are very irregular, and he is often absent.
Very strange. H
went back in jus
an hour?
No, sir, that is just impossible!
I better tell you who this person is. This is Inspector Newcomen of Scotland Yard.
Oh! Is Mr. Hyde in trouble! What has he done?
He doesn't seem to be a very popular character. And now, just let me and this gentleman have a look around.

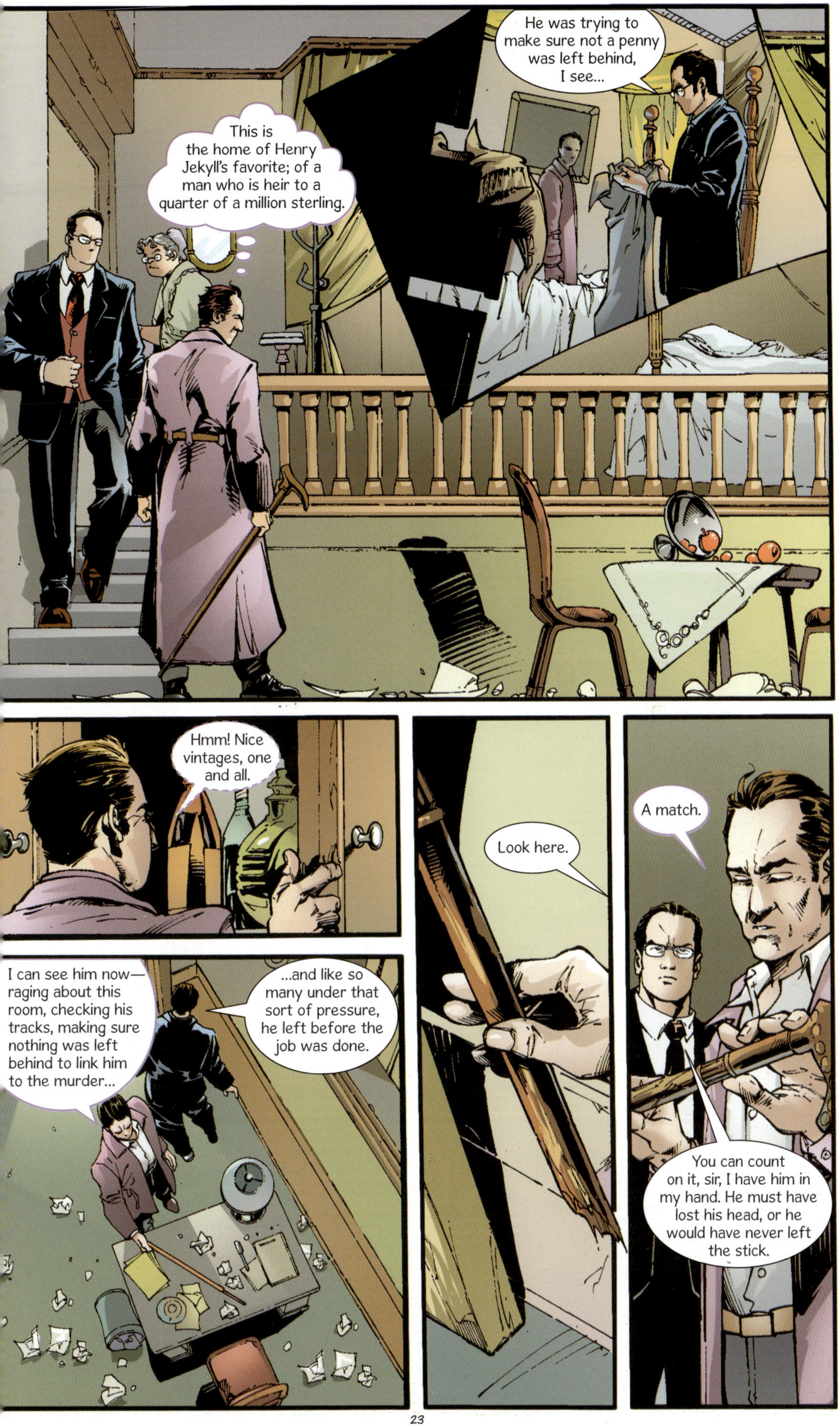
This is the home of Henry Jekyll's favorite; of a man who is heir to a quarter of a million sterling.
He was trying to make sure not a penny was left behind, I see...
Hmm! Nice vintages, one and all.
I can see him now—raging about this room, checking his tracks, making sure nothing was left behind to link him to the murder...
...and like so many under that sort of pressure, he left before the job was done.
Look here.
A match.
You can count on it, sir, I have him in my hand. He must have lost his head, or he would have never left the stick.

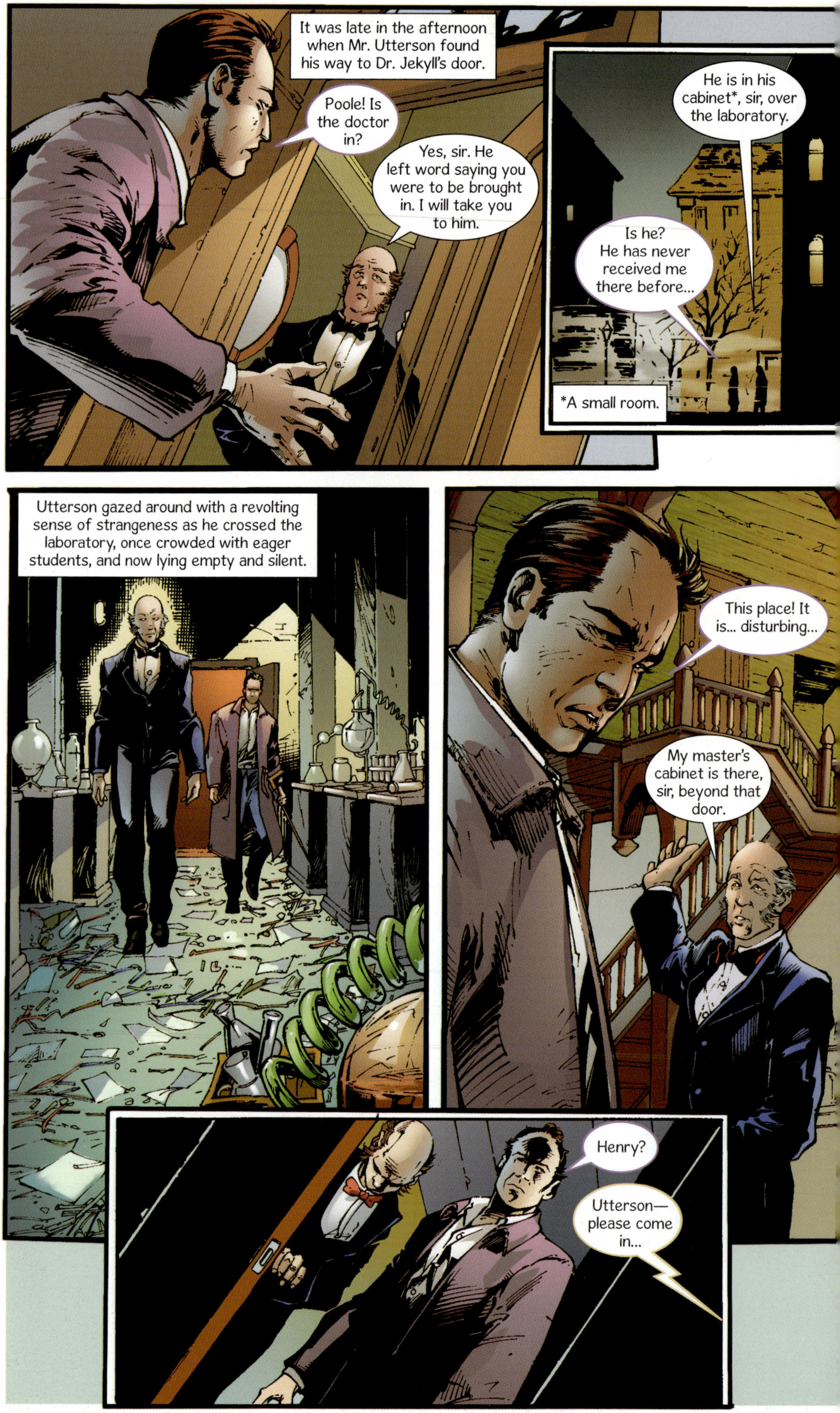
It was late in the afternoon when Mr. Utterson found his way to Dr. Jekyll's door.
Poole! Is the doctor in?
Yes, sir. He left word saying you were to be brought in. I will take you to him.
He is in his cabinet*, sir, over the laboratory.
Is he? He has never received me there before...
*A small room.
Utterson gazed around with a revolting sense of strangeness as he crossed the laboratory, once crowded with eager students, and now lying empty and silent.
This place! It is... disturbing...
My master's cabinet is there, sir, beyond that door.
Henry?
Utterson— please come in...

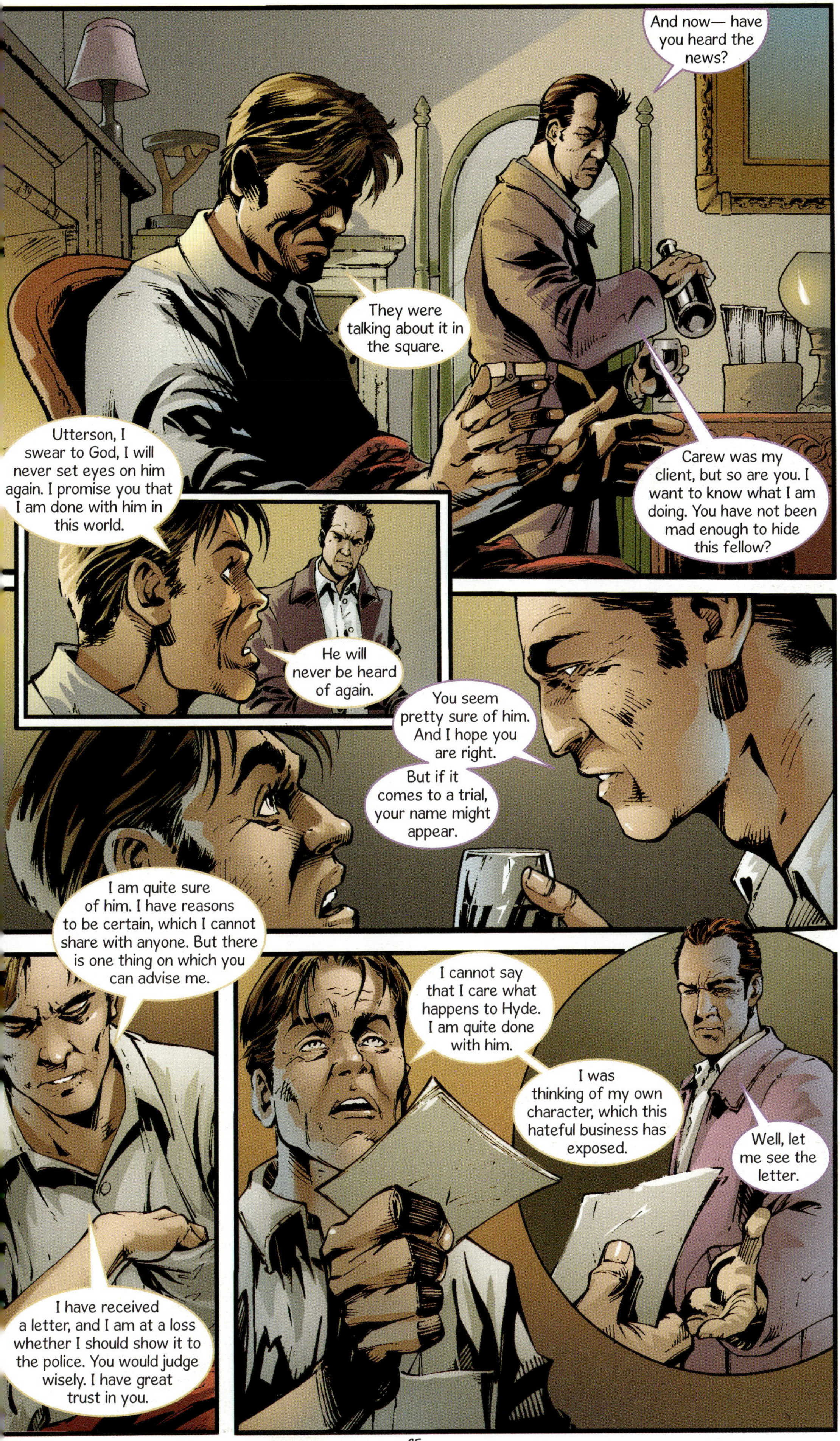
And now— have you heard the news?
They were talking about it in the square.
Carew was my client, but so are you. I want to know what I am doing. You have not been mad enough to hide this fellow?
Utterson, I swear to God, I will never set eyes on him again. I promise you that I am done with him in this world.
He will never be heard of again.
You seem pretty sure of him. And I hope you are right.
But if it comes to a trial, your name might appear.
I am quite sure of him. I have reasons to be certain, which I cannot share with anyone. But there is one thing on which you can advise me.
I have received a letter, and I am at a loss whether I should show it to the police. You would judge wisely. I have great trust in you.
I cannot say that I care what happens to Hyde. I am quite done with him.
I was thinking of my own character, which this hateful business has exposed.
Well, let me see the letter.

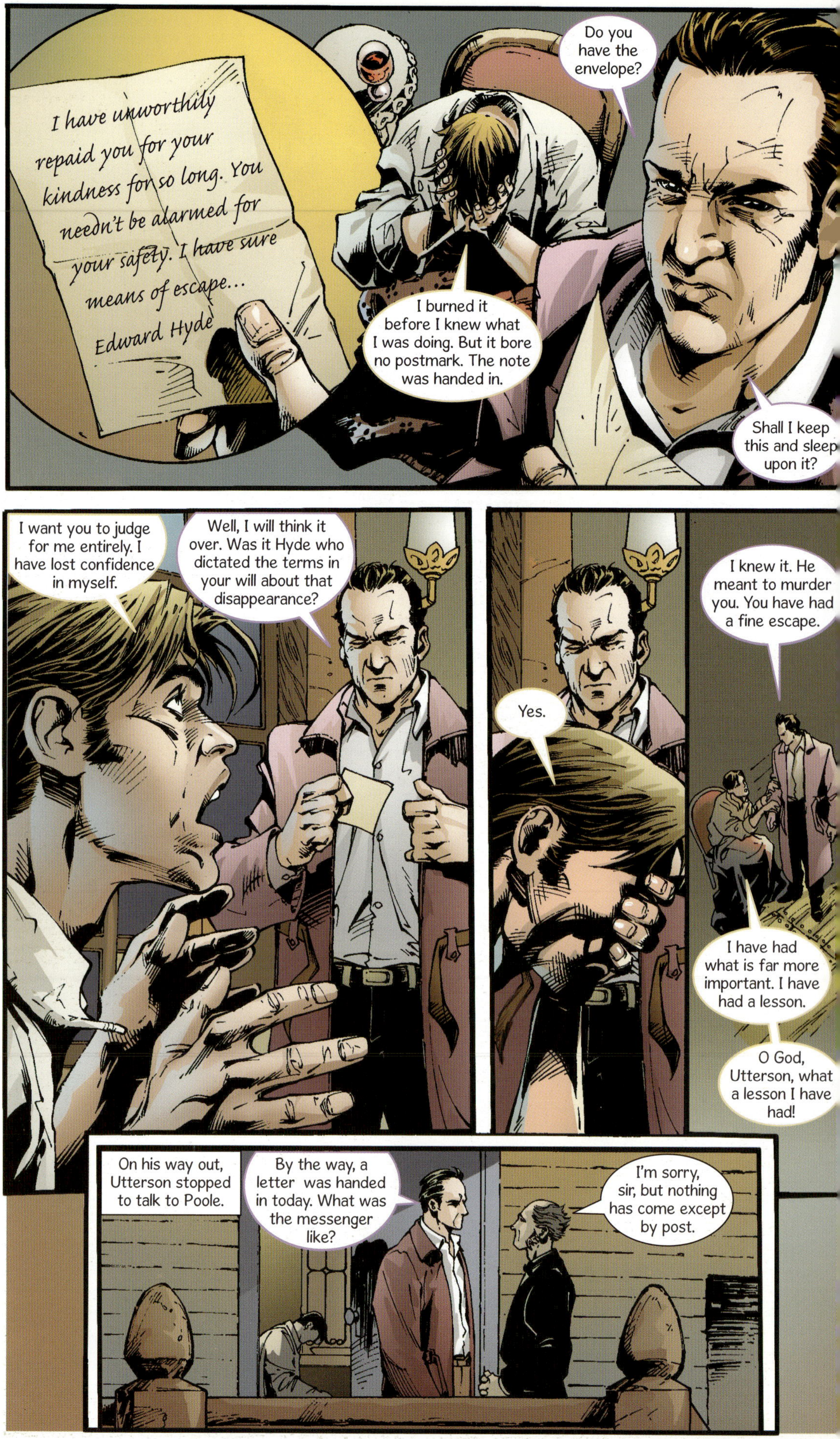
I have unworthily repaid you for your kindness for so long. You needn't be alarmed for your safety. I have sure means of escape... Edward Hyde
Do you have the envelope?
I burned it before I knew what I was doing. But it bore no postmark. The note was handed in.
Shall I keep this and sleep upon it?
I want you to judge for me entirely. I have lost confidence in myself.
Well, I will think it over. Was it Hyde who dictated the terms in your will about that disappearance?
Yes.
I knew it. He meant to murder you. You have had a fine escape.
I have had what is far more important. I have had a lesson.
O God, Utterson, what a lesson I have had!
On his way out, Utterson stopped to talk to Poole.
By the way, a letter was handed in today. What was the messenger like?
I'm sorry, sir, but nothing has come except by post.

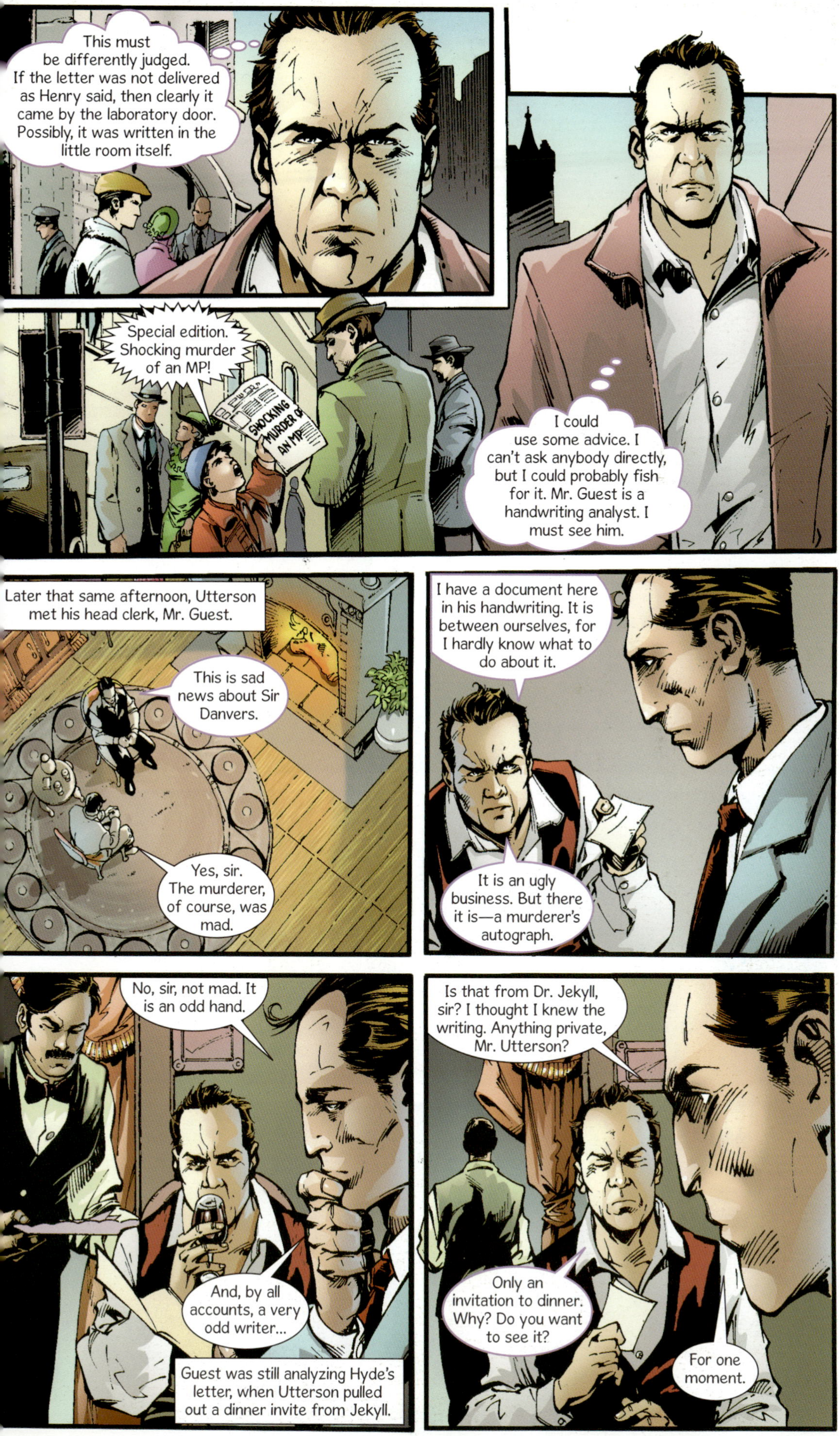

This must be differently judged. If the letter was not delivered as Henry said, then clearly it came by the laboratory door. Possibly, it was written in the little room itself.
Special edition. Shocking murder of an MP!
SHOCKING MURDER OF AN MP
I could use some advice. I can't ask anybody directly, but I could probably fish for it. Mr. Guest is a handwriting analyst. I must see him.
Later that same afternoon, Utterson met his head clerk, Mr. Guest.
This is sad news about Sir Danvers.
Yes, sir. The murderer, of course, was mad.
I have a document here in his handwriting. It is between ourselves, for I hardly know what to do about it.
It is an ugly business. But there it is—a murderer's autograph.
No, sir, not mad. It is an odd hand.
And, by all accounts, a very odd writer...
Guest was still analyzing Hyde's letter, when Utterson pulled out a dinner invite from Jekyll.
Is that from Dr. Jekyll, sir? I thought I knew the writing. Anything private, Mr. Utterson?
Only an invitation to dinner. Why? Do you want to see it?
For one moment.

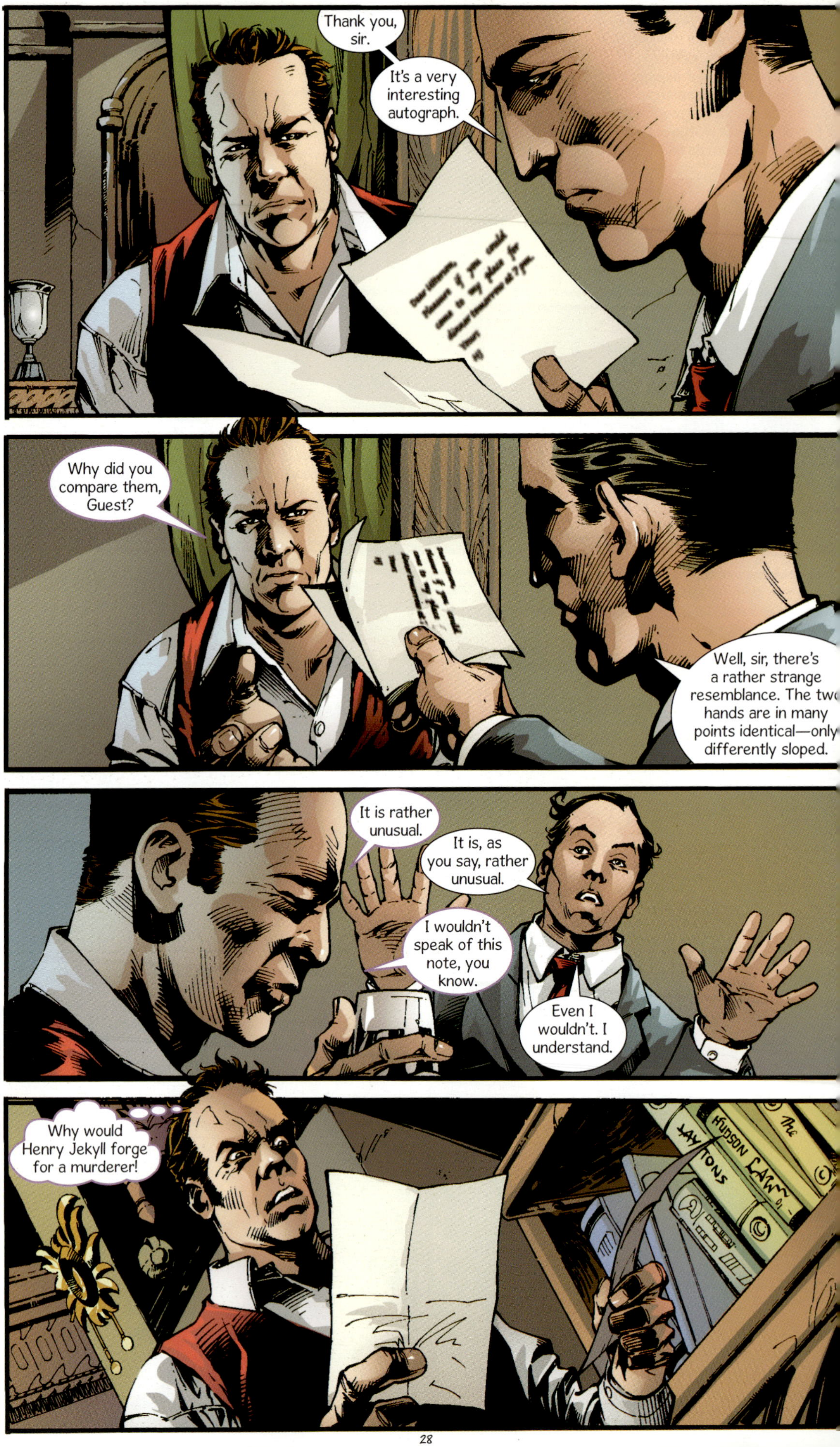
Thank you, sir.
It's a very interesting autograph.
Why did you compare them, Guest?
Well, sir, there's a rather strange resemblance. The tw hands are in many points identical—only differently sloped.
It is rather unusual.
It is, as you say, rather unusual.
I wouldn't speak of this note, you know.
Even I wouldn't. I understand.
Why would Henry Jekyll forge for a murderer!

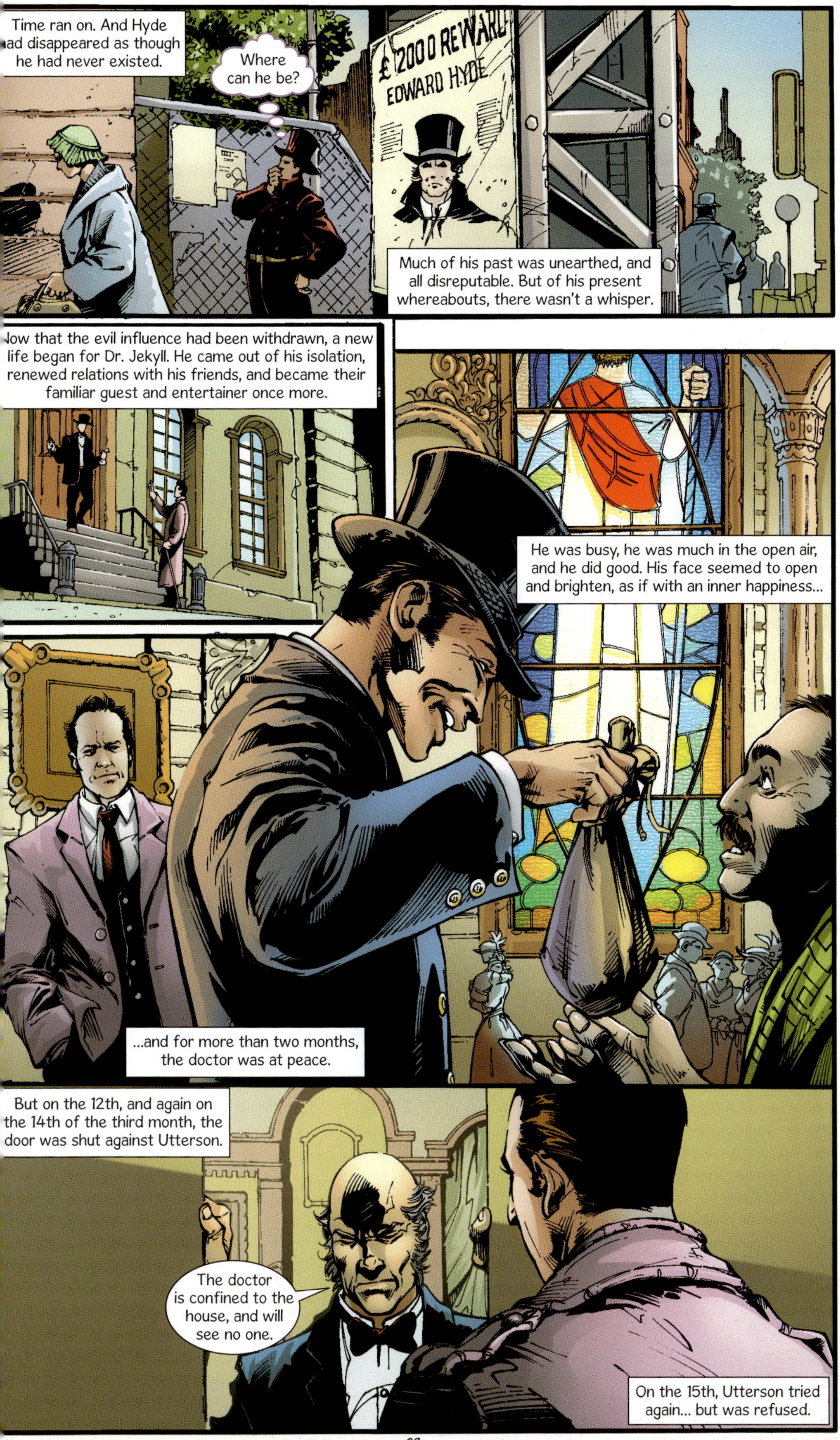

Time ran on. And Hyde had disappeared as though he had never existed.
Where can he be?
£2000 REWARD
EDWARD HYDE
Much of his past was unearthed, and all disreputable. But of his present whereabouts, there wasn't a whisper.
Now that the evil influence had been withdrawn, a new life began for Dr. Jekyll. He came out of his isolation, renewed relations with his friends, and became their familiar guest and entertainer once more.
He was busy, he was much in the open air, and he did good. His face seemed to open and brighten, as if with an inner happiness...
...and for more than two months, the doctor was at peace.
But on the 12th, and again on the 14th of the third month, the door was shut against Utterson.
The doctor is confined to the house, and will see no one.
On the 15th, Utterson tried again... but was refused.

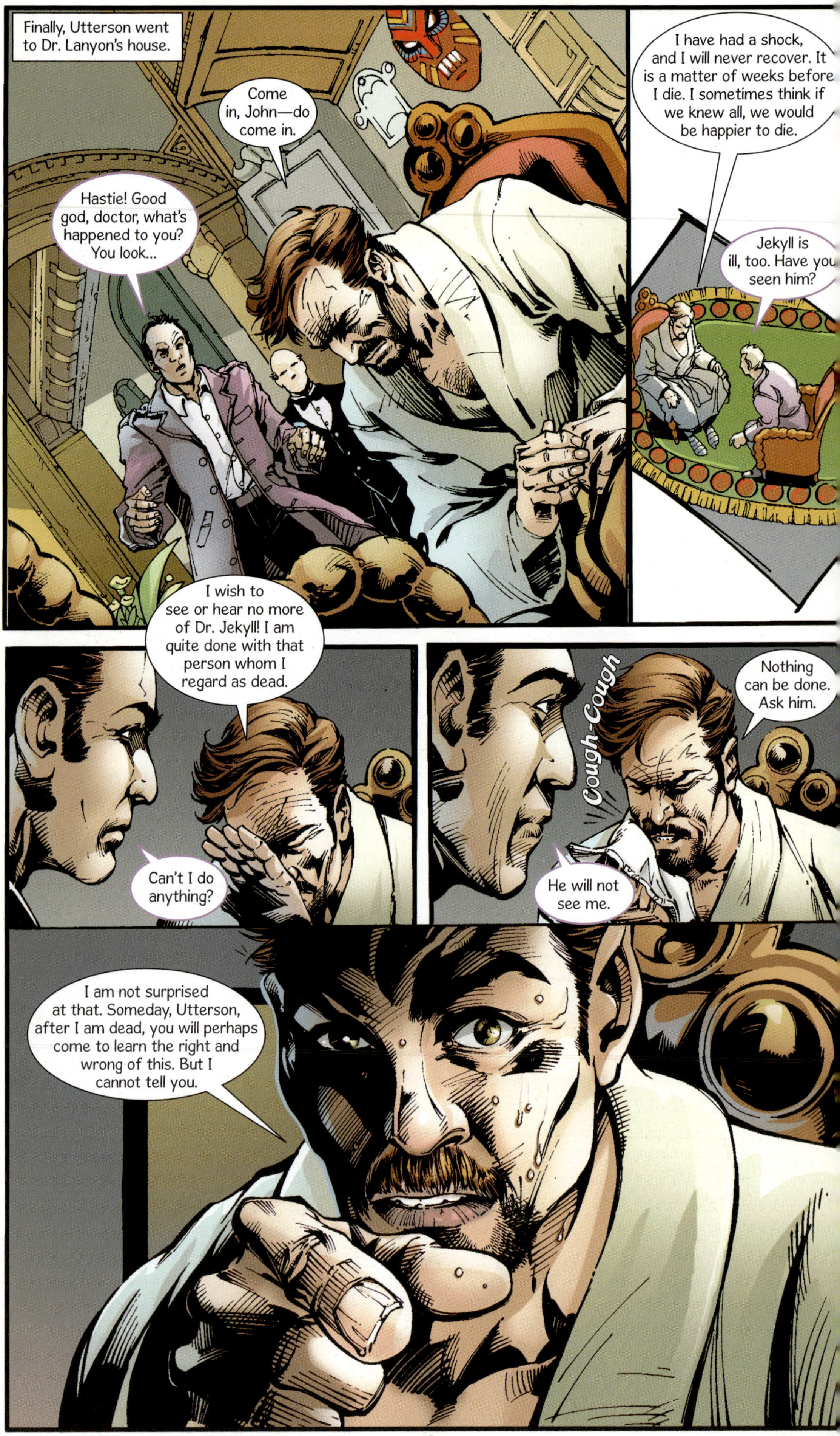
Finally, Utterson went to Dr. Lanyon's house.
Come in, John—do come in.
Hastie! Good god, doctor, what's happened to you? You look...
I have had a shock, and I will never recover. It is a matter of weeks before I die. I sometimes think if we knew all, we would be happier to die.
Jekyll is ill, too. Have you seen him?
I wish to see or hear no more of Dr. Jekyll! I am quite done with that person whom I regard as dead.
Can't I do anything?
Nothing can be done. Ask him.
Cough-Cough
He will not see me.
I am not surprised at that. Someday, Utterson, after I am dead, you will perhaps come to learn the right and wrong of this. But I cannot tell you.

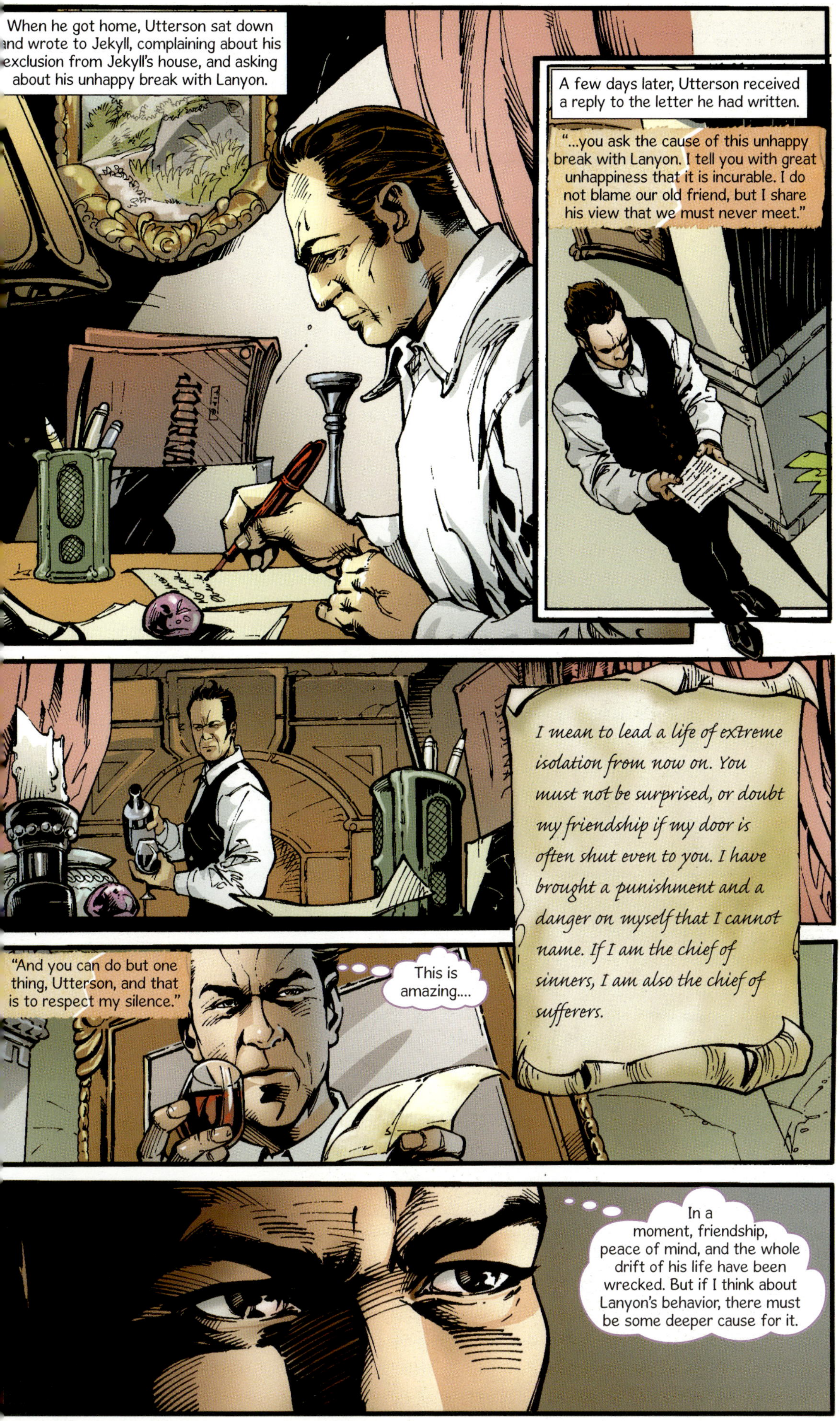

When he got home, Utterson sat down and wrote to Jekyll, complaining about his exclusion from Jekyll's house, and asking about his unhappy break with Lanyon.
JOURNAL
A few days later, Utterson received a reply to the letter he had written.
"...you ask the cause of this unhappy break with Lanyon. I tell you with great unhappiness that it is incurable. I do not blame our old friend, but I share his view that we must never meet."
I mean to lead a life of extreme isolation from now on. You must not be surprised, or doubt my friendship if my door is often shut even to you. I have brought a punishment and a danger on myself that I cannot name. If I am the chief of sinners, I am also the chief of sufferers.
"And you can do but one thing, Utterson, and that is to respect my silence."
This is amazing....
In a moment, friendship, peace of mind, and the whole drift of his life have been wrecked. But if I think about Lanyon's behavior, there must be some deeper cause for it.

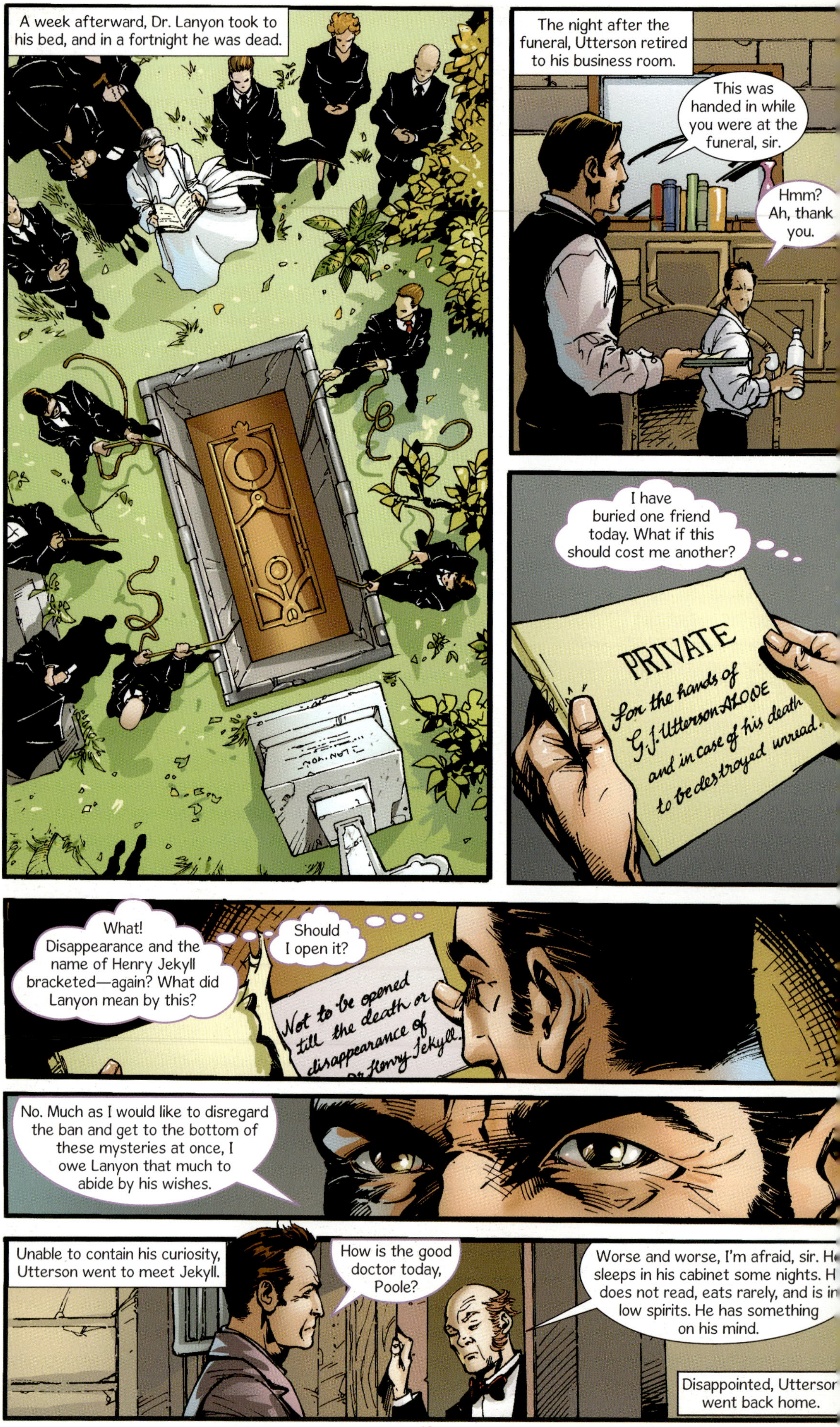
A week afterward, Dr. Lanyon took to his bed, and in a fortnight he was dead.
The night after the funeral, Utterson retired to his business room.
This was handed in while you were at the funeral, sir.
Hmm? Ah, thank you.
I have buried one friend today. What if this should cost me another?
PRIVATE
For the hands of G.J. Utterson ALONE and in case of his death to be destroyed unread.
What! Disappearance and the name of Henry Jekyll bracketed—again? What did Lanyon mean by this?
Should I open it?
Not to be opened till the death or disappearance of
No. Much as I would like to disregard the ban and get to the bottom of these mysteries at once, I owe Lanyon that much to abide by his wishes.
Unable to contain his curiosity, Utterson went to meet Jekyll.
How is the good doctor today, Poole?
Worse and worse, I'm afraid, sir. He sleeps in his cabinet some nights. He does not read, eats rarely, and is in low spirits. He has something on his mind.
Disappointed, Utterson went back home.

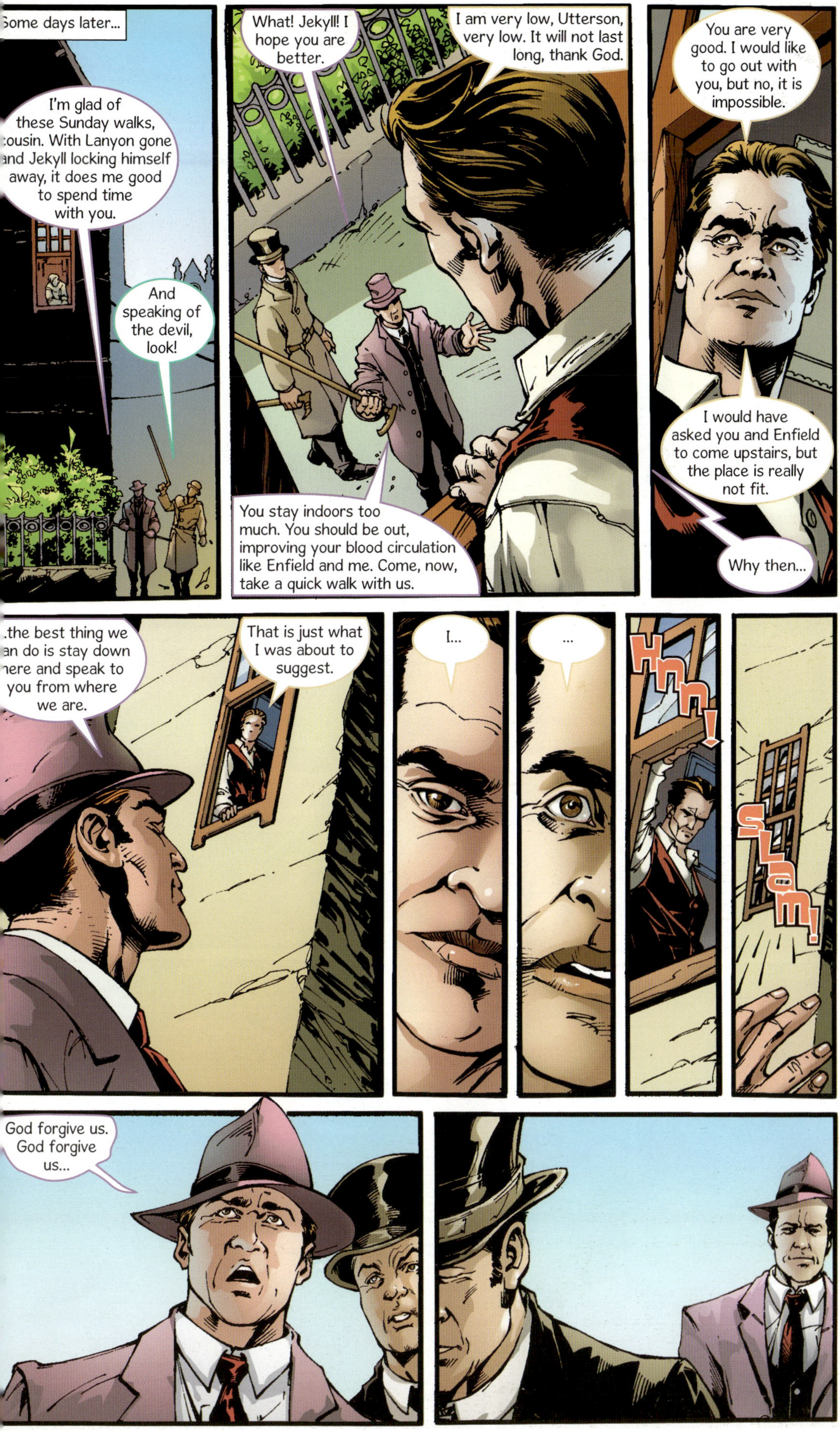

Some days later...
I'm glad of these Sunday walks, cousin. With Lanyon gone and Jekyll locking himself away, it does me good to spend time with you.
And speaking of the devil, look!
What! Jekyll! I hope you are better.
I am very low, Utterson, very low. It will not last long, thank God.
You stay indoors too much. You should be out, improving your blood circulation like Enfield and me. Come, now, take a quick walk with us.
You are very good. I would like to go out with you, but no, it is impossible.
I would have asked you and Enfield to come upstairs, but the place is really not fit.
Why then...
...the best thing we can do is stay down here and speak to you from where we are.
That is just what I was about to suggest.
I...
...
HNN!
SLAM!
God forgive us. God forgive us...

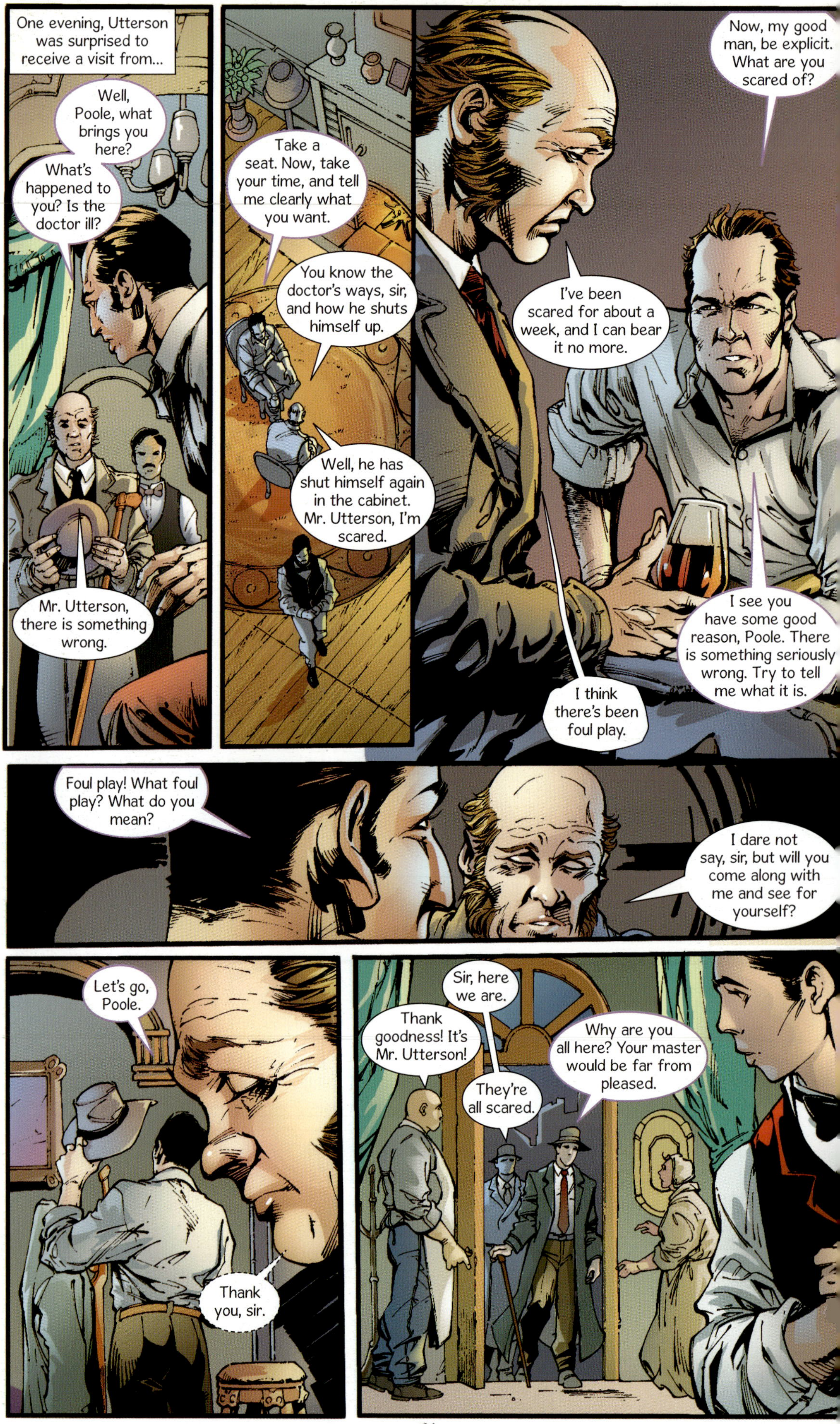
One evening, Utterson was surprised to receive a visit from...
Well, Poole, what brings you here?
What's happened to you? Is the doctor ill?
Mr. Utterson, there is something wrong.
Take a seat. Now, take your time, and tell me clearly what you want.
You know the doctor's ways, sir, and how he shuts himself up.
Well, he has shut himself again in the cabinet. Mr. Utterson, I'm scared.
Now, my good man, be explicit. What are you scared of?
I've been scared for about a week, and I can bear it no more.
I see you have some good reason, Poole. There is something seriously wrong. Try to tell me what it is.
I think there's been foul play.
Foul play! What foul play? What do you mean?
I dare not say, sir, but will you come along with me and see for yourself?
Let's go, Poole.
Thank you, sir.
Sir, here we are.
Thank goodness! It's Mr. Utterson!
They're all scared.
Why are you all here? Your master would be far from pleased.

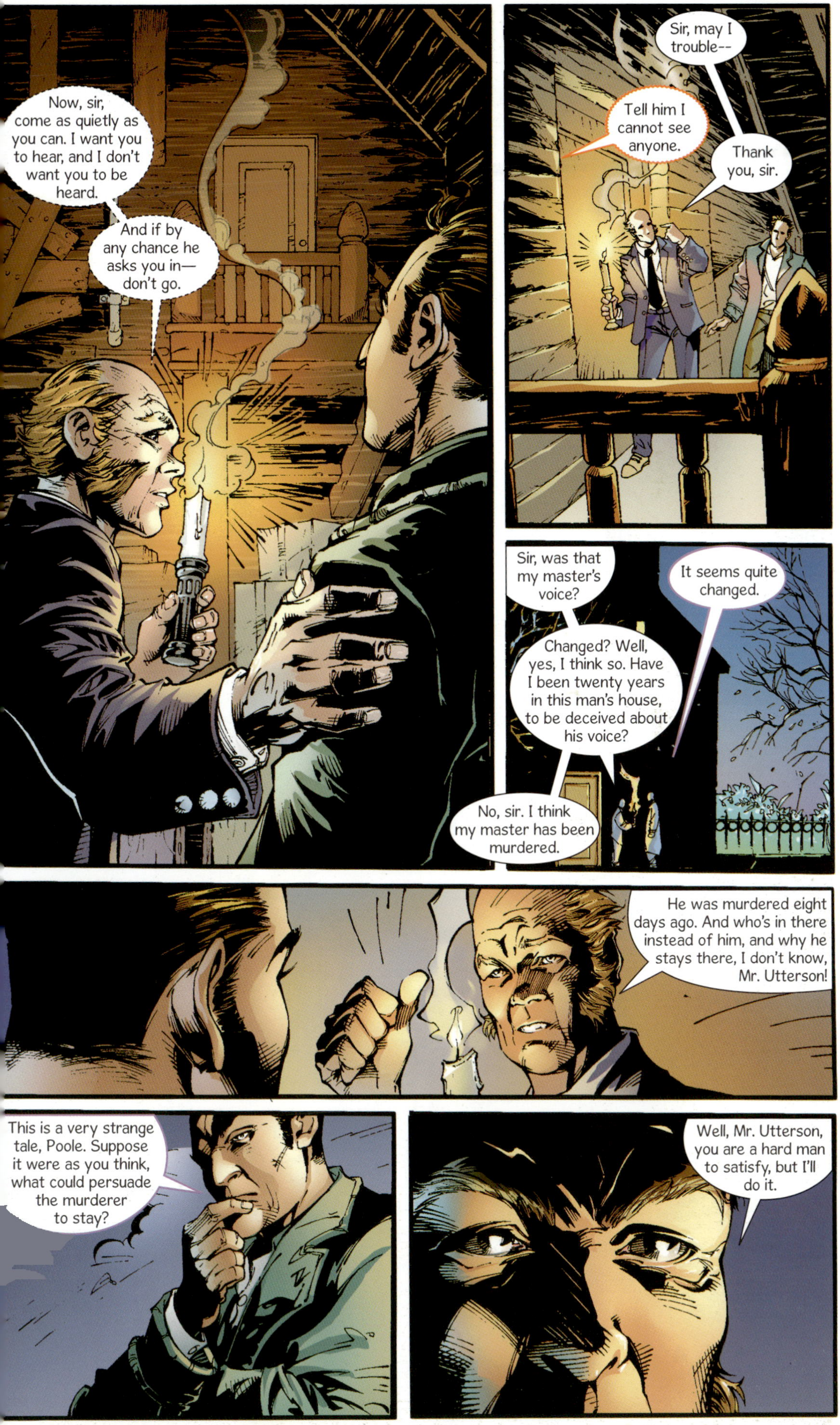
Now, sir, come as quietly as you can. I want you to hear, and I don't want you to be heard.
And if by any chance he asks you in— don't go.
Sir, may I trouble--
Tell him I cannot see anyone.
Thank you, sir.
Sir, was that my master's voice?
It seems quite changed.
Changed? Well, yes, I think so. Have I been twenty years in this man's house, to be deceived about his voice?
No, sir. I think my master has been murdered.
He was murdered eight days ago. And who's in there instead of him, and why he stays there, I don't know, Mr. Utterson!
This is a very strange tale, Poole. Suppose it were as you think, what could persuade the murderer to stay?
Well, Mr. Utterson, you are a hard man to satisfy, but I'll do it.

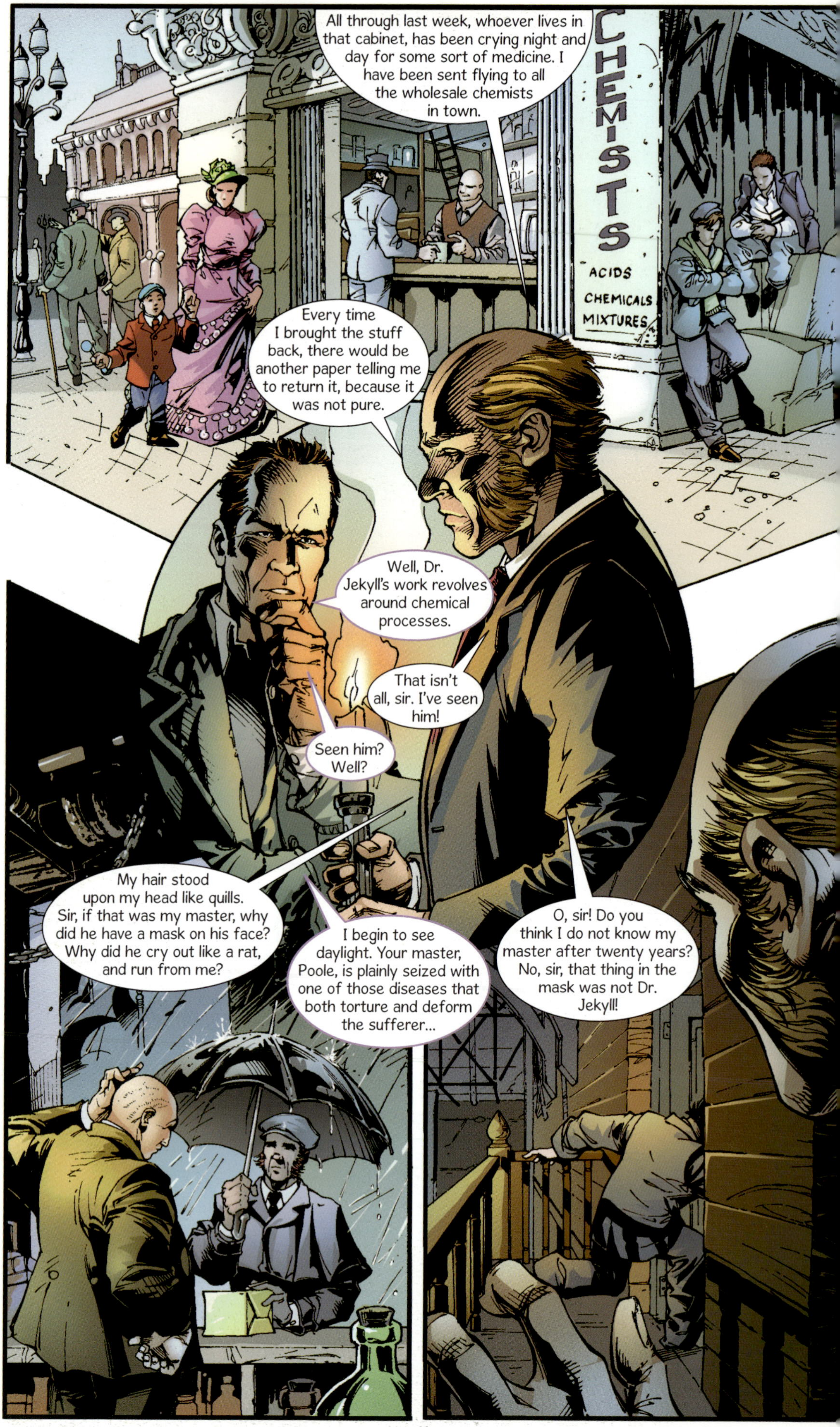
All through last week, whoever lives in that cabinet, has been crying night and day for some sort of medicine. I have been sent flying to all the wholesale chemists in town.
CHEMISTS
ACIDS
CHEMICALS
MIXTURES
Every time I brought the stuff back, there would be another paper telling me to return it, because it was not pure.
Well, Dr. Jekyll's work revolves around chemical processes.
That isn't all, sir. I've seen him!
Seen him? Well?
My hair stood upon my head like quills. Sir, if that was my master, why did he have a mask on his face? Why did he cry out like a rat, and run from me?
I begin to see daylight. Your master, Poole, is plainly seized with one of those diseases that both torture and deform the sufferer...
O, sir! Do you think I do not know my master after twenty years? No, sir, that thing in the mask was not Dr. Jekyll!

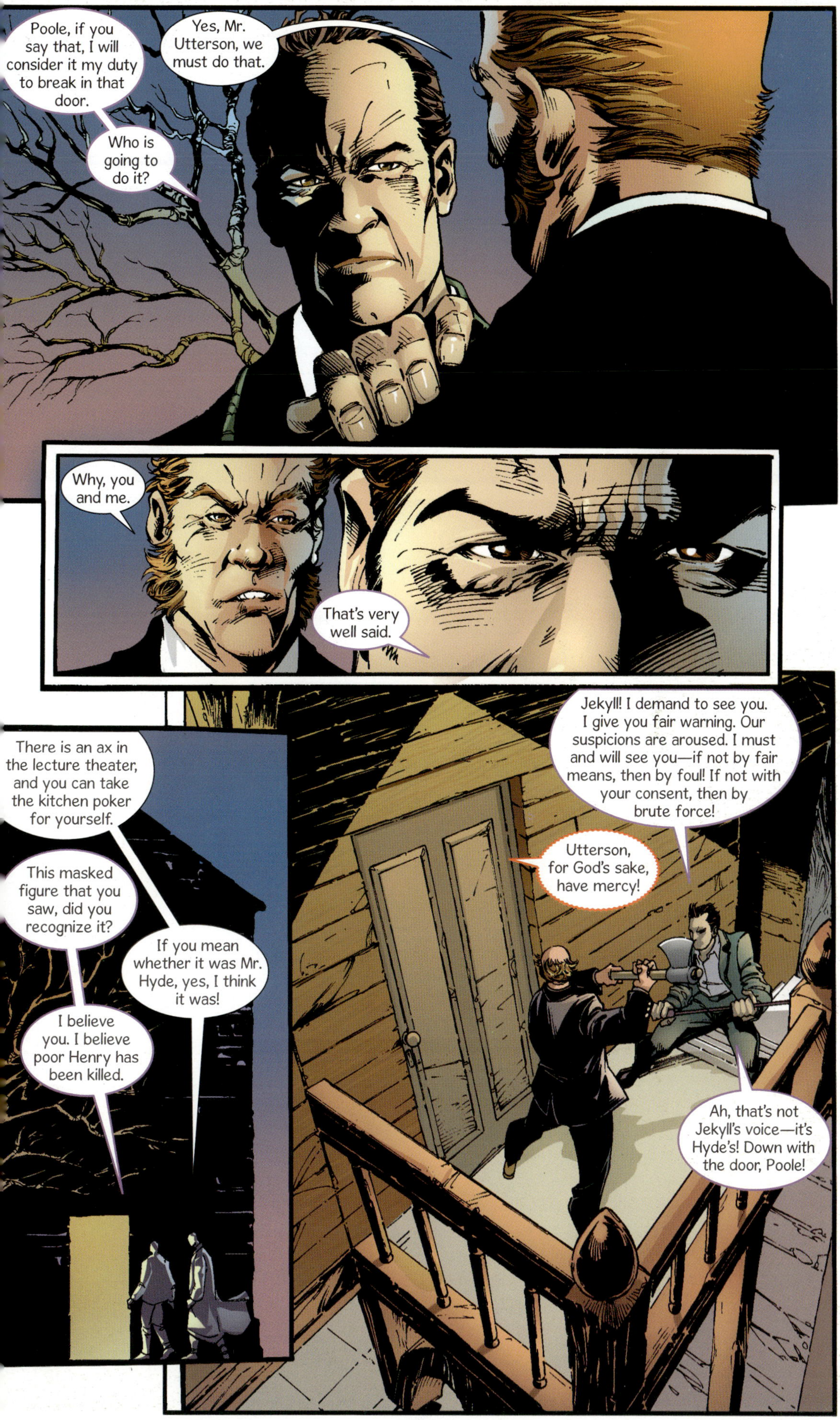
Poole, if you say that, I will consider it my duty to break in that door.
Yes, Mr. Utterson, we must do that.
Who is going to do it?
Why, you and me.
That's very well said.
There is an ax in the lecture theater, and you can take the kitchen poker for yourself.
This masked figure that you saw, did you recognize it?
If you mean whether it was Mr. Hyde, yes, I think it was!
I believe you. I believe poor Henry has been killed.
Jekyll! I demand to see you. I give you fair warning. Our suspicions are aroused. I must and will see you—if not by fair means, then by foul! If not with your consent, then by brute force!
Utterson, for God's sake, have mercy!
Ah, that's not Jekyll's voice—it's Hyde's! Down with the door, Poole!

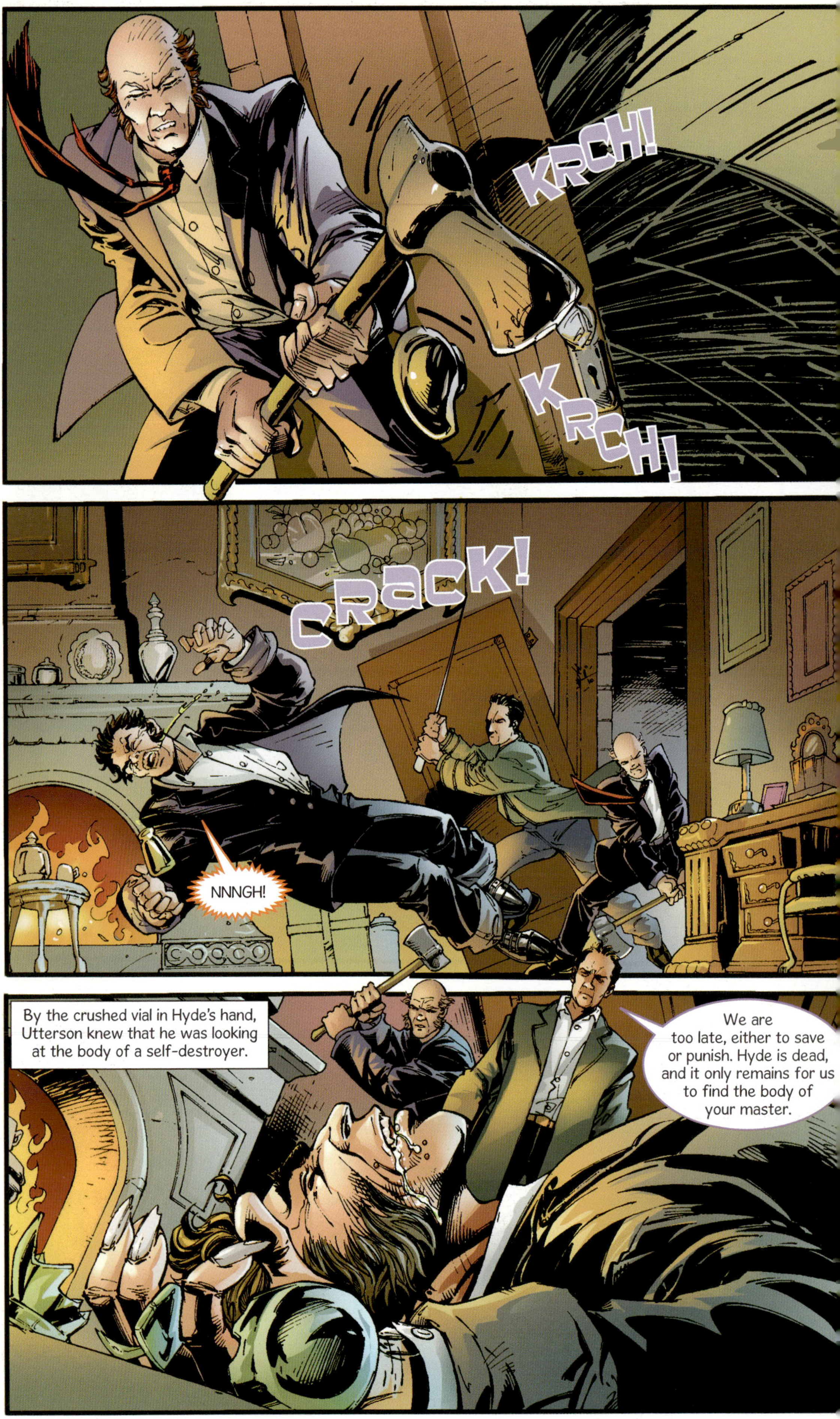
KRCH!
KRCH!
CRACK!
NNNGH!
By the crushed vial in Hyde's hand, Utterson knew that he was looking at the body of a self-destroyer.
We are too late, either to save or punish. Hyde is dead, and it only remains for us to find the body of your master.

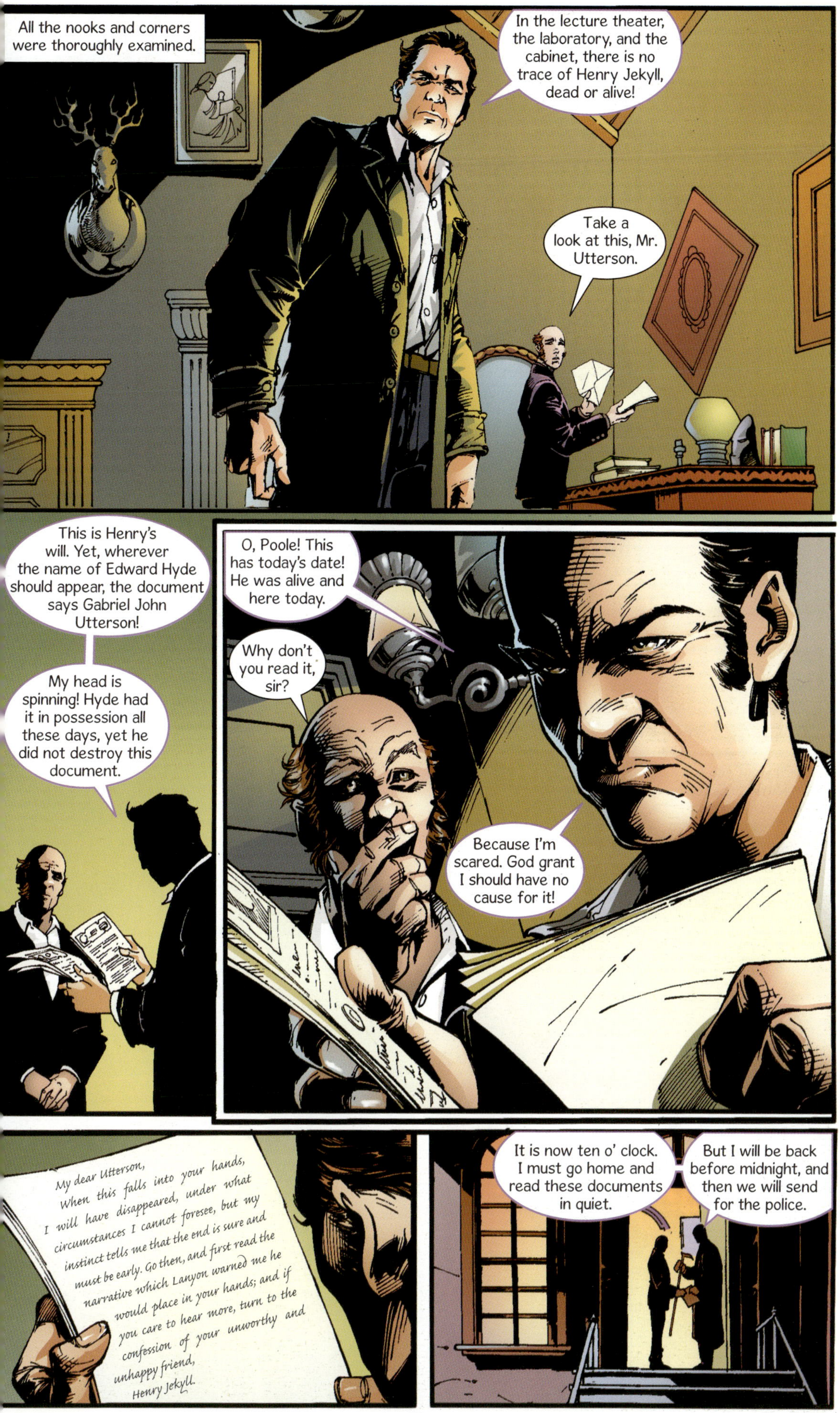
All the nooks and corners were thoroughly examined.
In the lecture theater, the laboratory, and the cabinet, there is no trace of Henry Jekyll, dead or alive!
Take a look at this, Mr. Utterson.
This is Henry's will. Yet, wherever the name of Edward Hyde should appear, the document says Gabriel John Utterson!
My head is spinning! Hyde had it in possession all these days, yet he did not destroy this document.
O, Poole! This has today's date! He was alive and here today.
Why don't you read it, sir?
Because I'm scared. God grant I should have no cause for it!
My dear Utterson,
When this falls into your hands, I will have disappeared, under what circumstances I cannot foresee, but my instinct tells me that the end is sure and must be early. Go then, and first read the narrative which Lanyon warned me he would place in your hands; and if you care to hear more, turn to the confession of your unworthy and unhappy friend,
Henry Jekyll.
It is now ten o' clock. I must go home and read these documents in quiet.
But I will be back before midnight, and then we will send for the police.

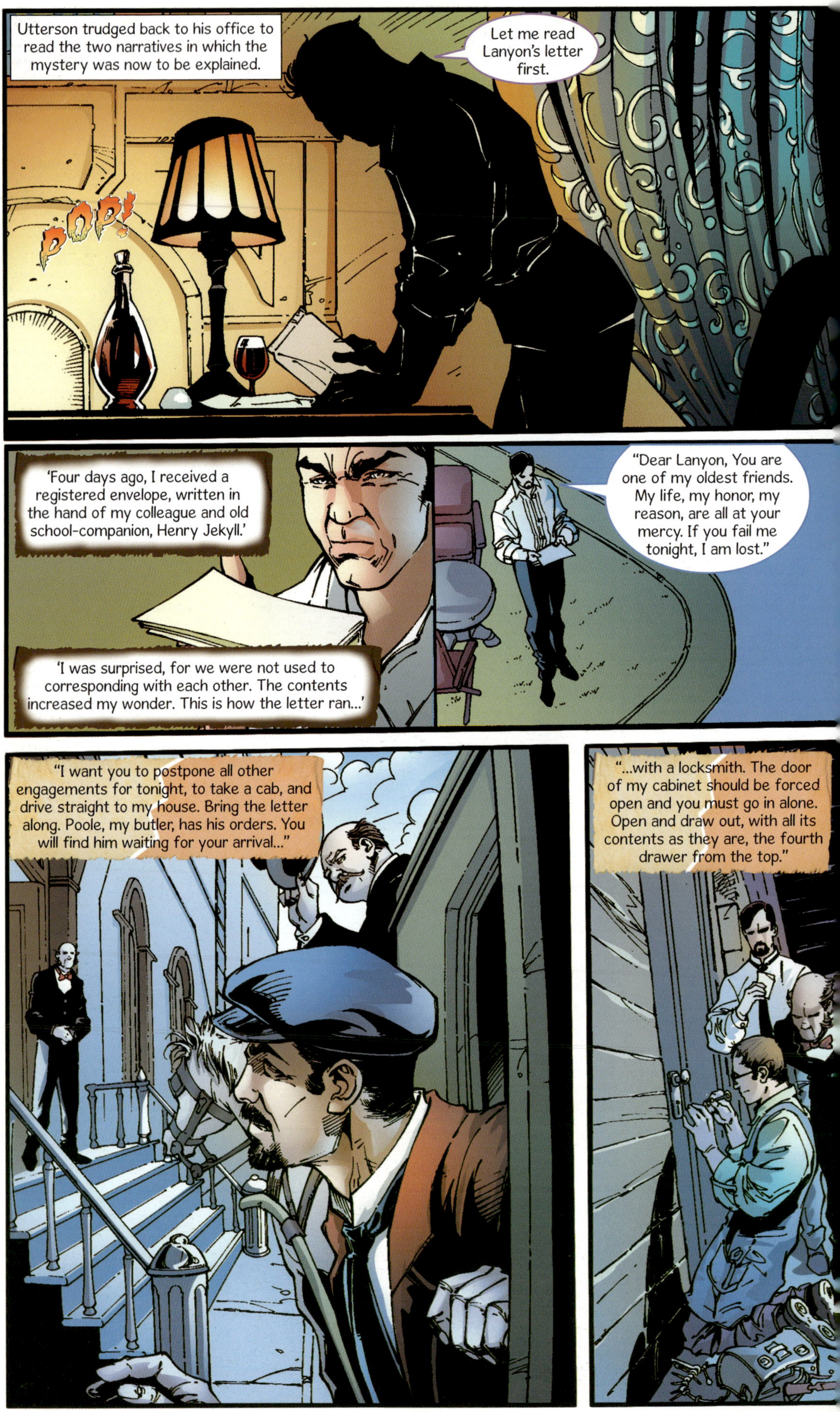
Utterson trudged back to his office to read the two narratives in which the mystery was now to be explained.
Let me read Lanyon's letter first.
POP!
'Four days ago, I received a registered envelope, written in the hand of my colleague and old school-companion, Henry Jekyll.'
'I was surprised, for we were not used to corresponding with each other. The contents increased my wonder. This is how the letter ran...'
"Dear Lanyon, You are one of my oldest friends. My life, my honor, my reason, are all at your mercy. If you fail me tonight, I am lost."
"I want you to postpone all other engagements for tonight, to take a cab, and drive straight to my house. Bring the letter along. Poole, my butler, has his orders. You will find him waiting for your arrival..."
"...with a locksmith. The door of my cabinet should be forced open and you must go in alone. Open and draw out, with all its contents as they are, the fourth drawer from the top."

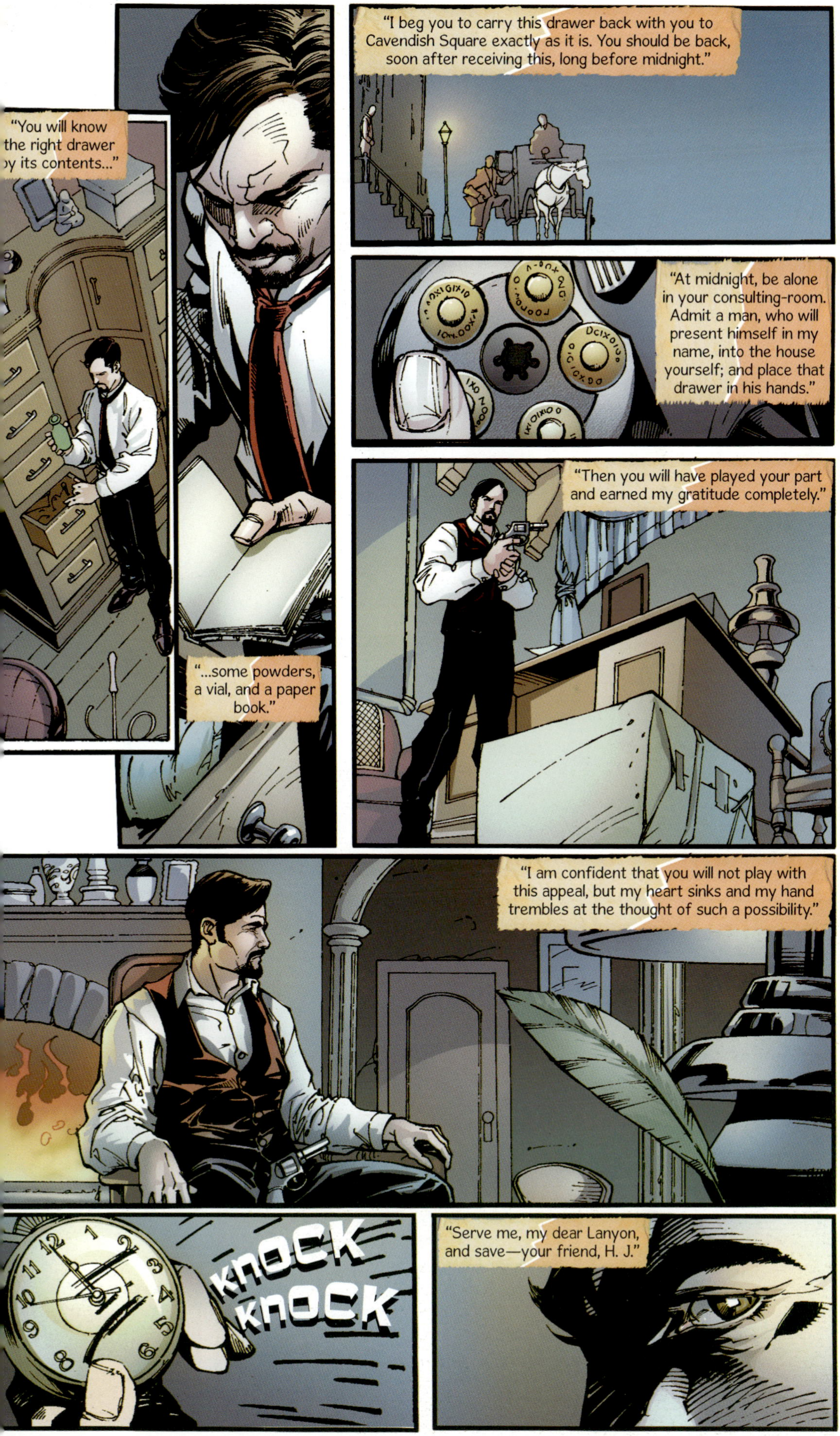

"You will know the right drawer by its contents..."
"...some powders, a vial, and a paper book."
"I beg you to carry this drawer back with you to Cavendish Square exactly as it is. You should be back, soon after receiving this, long before midnight."
"At midnight, be alone in your consulting-room. Admit a man, who will present himself in my name, into the house yourself; and place that drawer in his hands."
"Then you will have played your part and earned my gratitude completely."
"I am confident that you will not play with this appeal, but my heart sinks and my hand trembles at the thought of such a possibility."
KNOCK KNOCK
"Serve me, my dear Lanyon, and save—your friend, H. J."

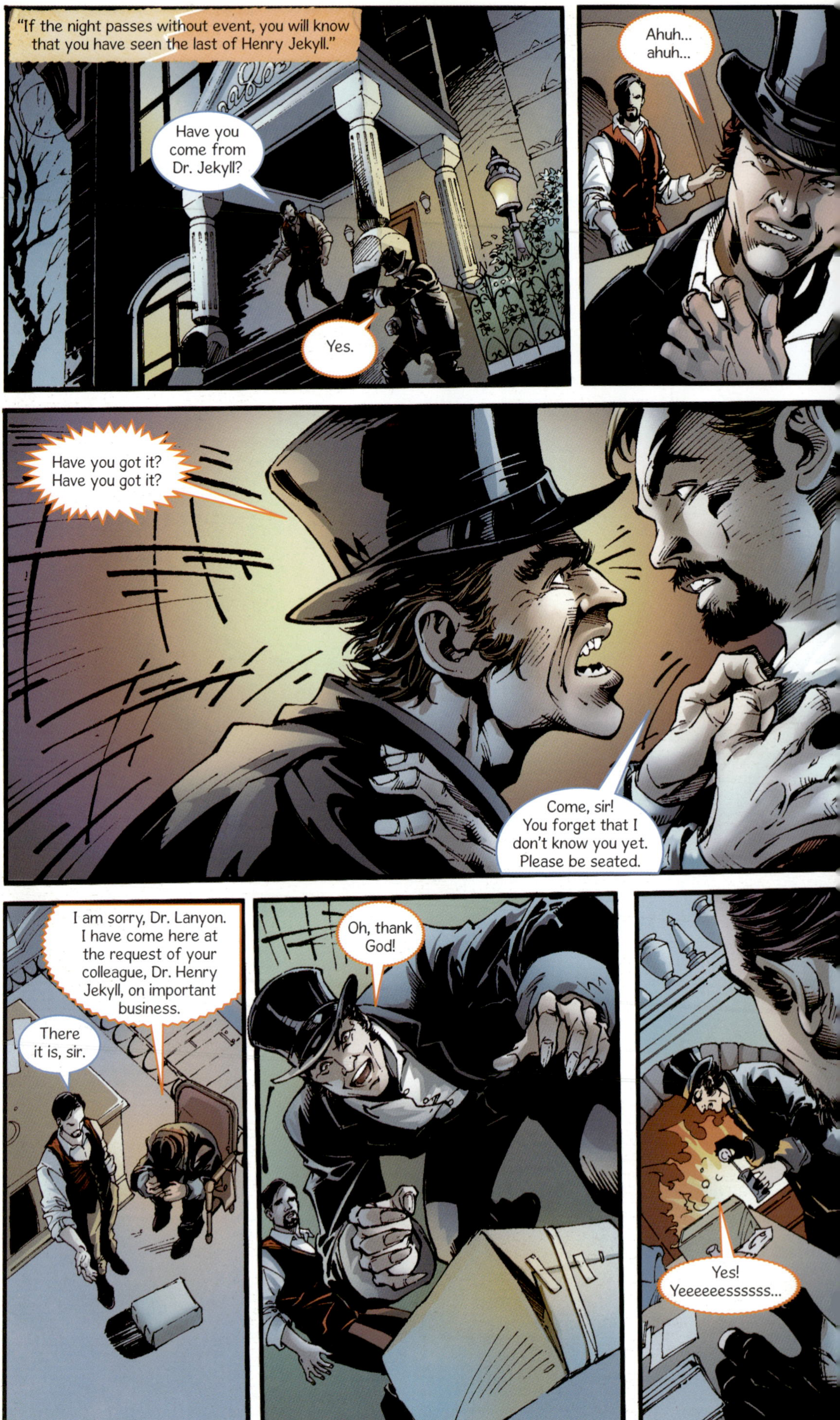
"If the night passes without event, you will know that you have seen the last of Henry Jekyll."
Have you come from Dr. Jekyll?
Yes.
Ahuh... ahuh...
Have you got it? Have you got it?
Come, sir! You forget that I don't know you yet. Please be seated.
I am sorry, Dr. Lanyon. I have come here at the request of your colleague, Dr. Henry Jekyll, on important business.
There it is, sir.
Oh, thank God!
Yes! Yeeeeeessssss...

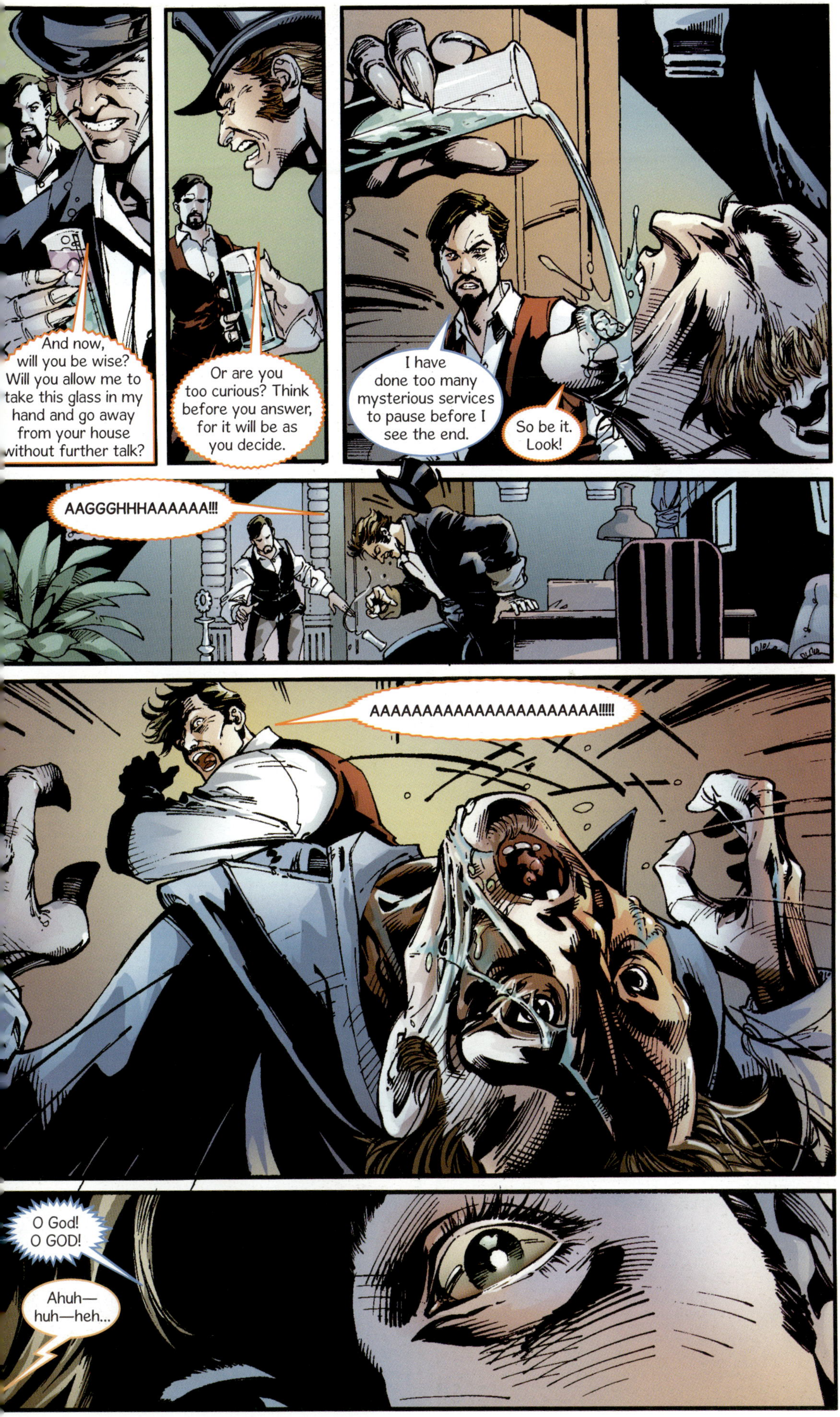
And now, will you be wise? Will you allow me to take this glass in my hand and go away from your house without further talk?
Or are you too curious? Think before you answer, for it will be as you decide.
I have done too many mysterious services to pause before I see the end.
So be it. Look!
AAGGGHHHAAAAAA!!!
AAAAAAAAAAAAAAAAAAAAA!!!!
O God! O GOD!
Ahuh—huh—heh...

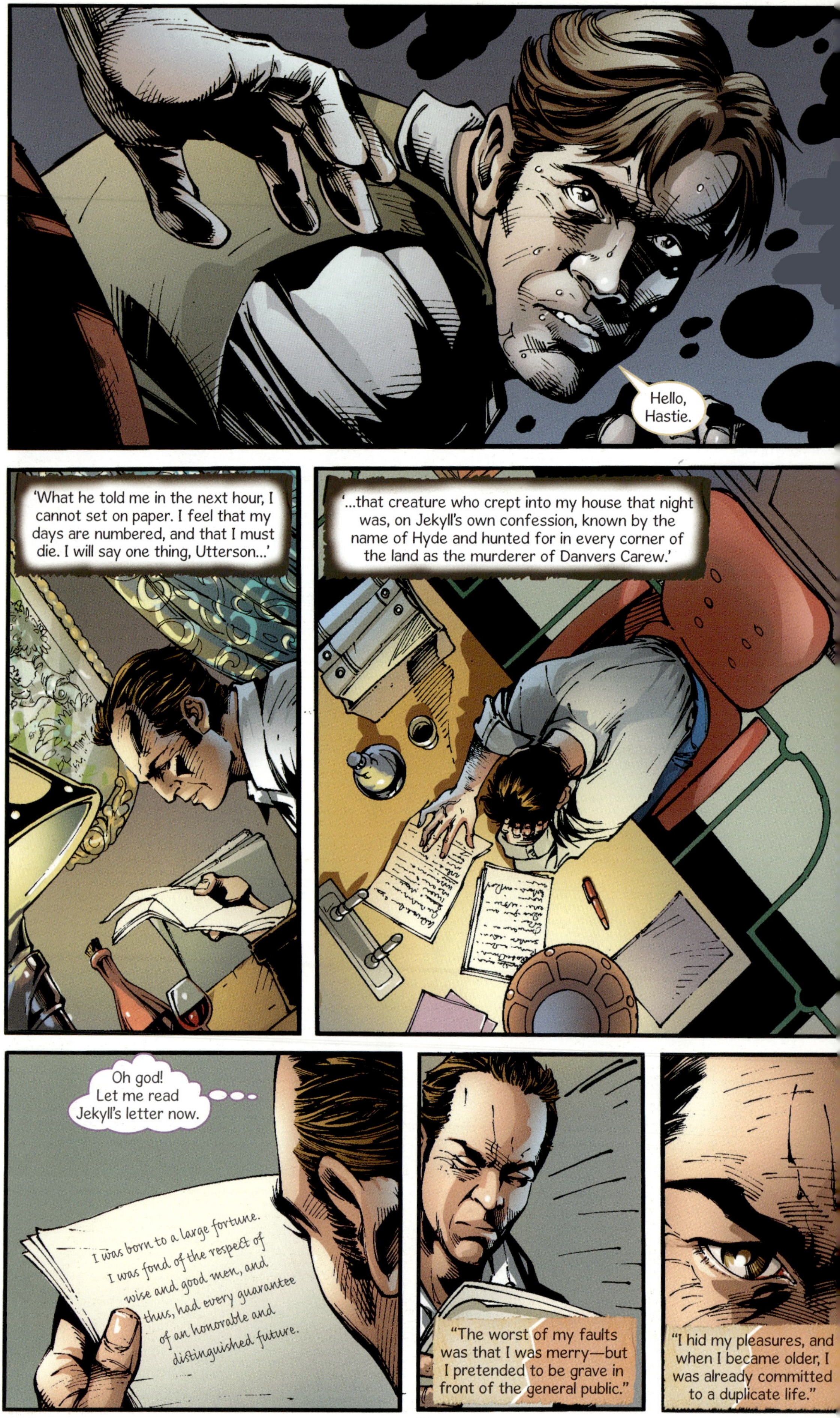
Hello, Hastie.
'What he told me in the next hour, I cannot set on paper. I feel that my days are numbered, and that I must die. I will say one thing, Utterson...'
'...that creature who crept into my house that night was, on Jekyll's own confession, known by the name of Hyde and hunted for in every corner of the land as the murderer of Danvers Carew.'
Oh god! Let me read Jekyll's letter now.
I was born to a large fortune. I was fond of the respect of wise and good men, and thus, had every guarantee of an honorable and distinguished future.
"The worst of my faults was that I was merry—but I pretended to be grave in front of the general public."
"I hid my pleasures, and when I became older, I was already committed to a duplicate life."

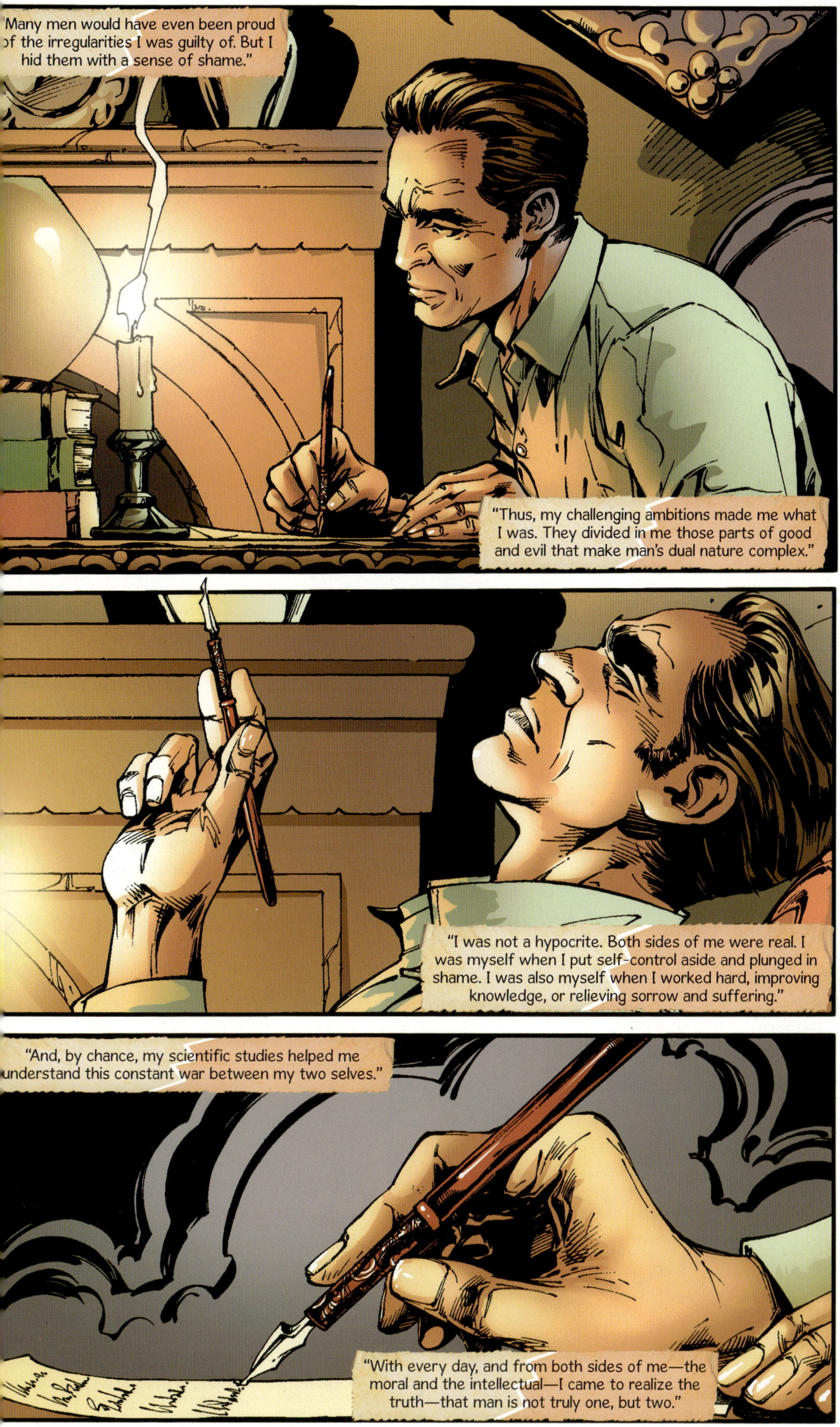
"Many men would have even been proud of the irregularities I was guilty of. But I hid them with a sense of shame."
"Thus, my challenging ambitions made me what I was. They divided in me those parts of good and evil that make man's dual nature complex."
"I was not a hypocrite. Both sides of me were real. I was myself when I put self-control aside and plunged in shame. I was also myself when I worked hard, improving knowledge, or relieving sorrow and suffering."
"And, by chance, my scientific studies helped me understand this constant war between my two selves."
"With every day, and from both sides of me—the moral and the intellectual—I came to realize the truth—that man is not truly one, but two."

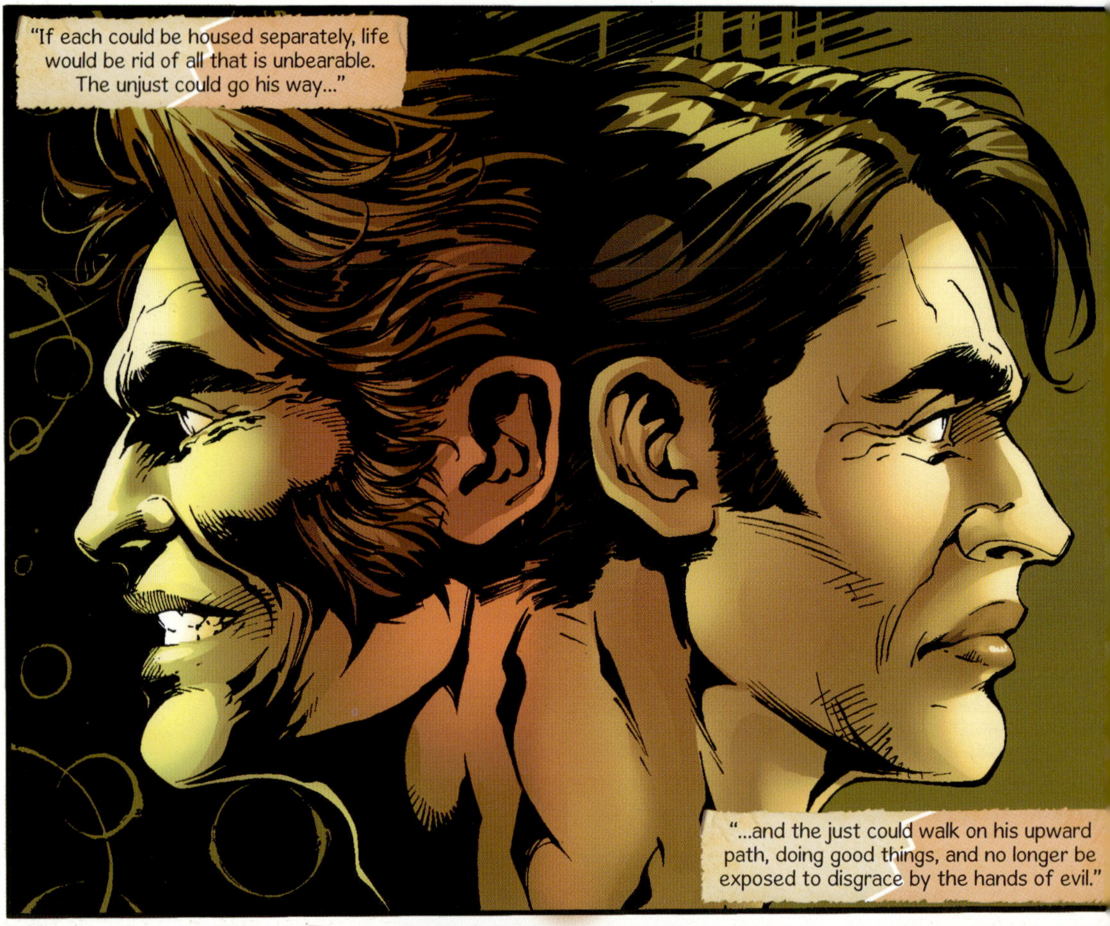
"If each could be housed separately, life would be rid of all that is unbearable. The unjust could go his way..."
"...and the just could walk on his upward path, doing good things, and no longer be exposed to disgrace by the hands of evil."

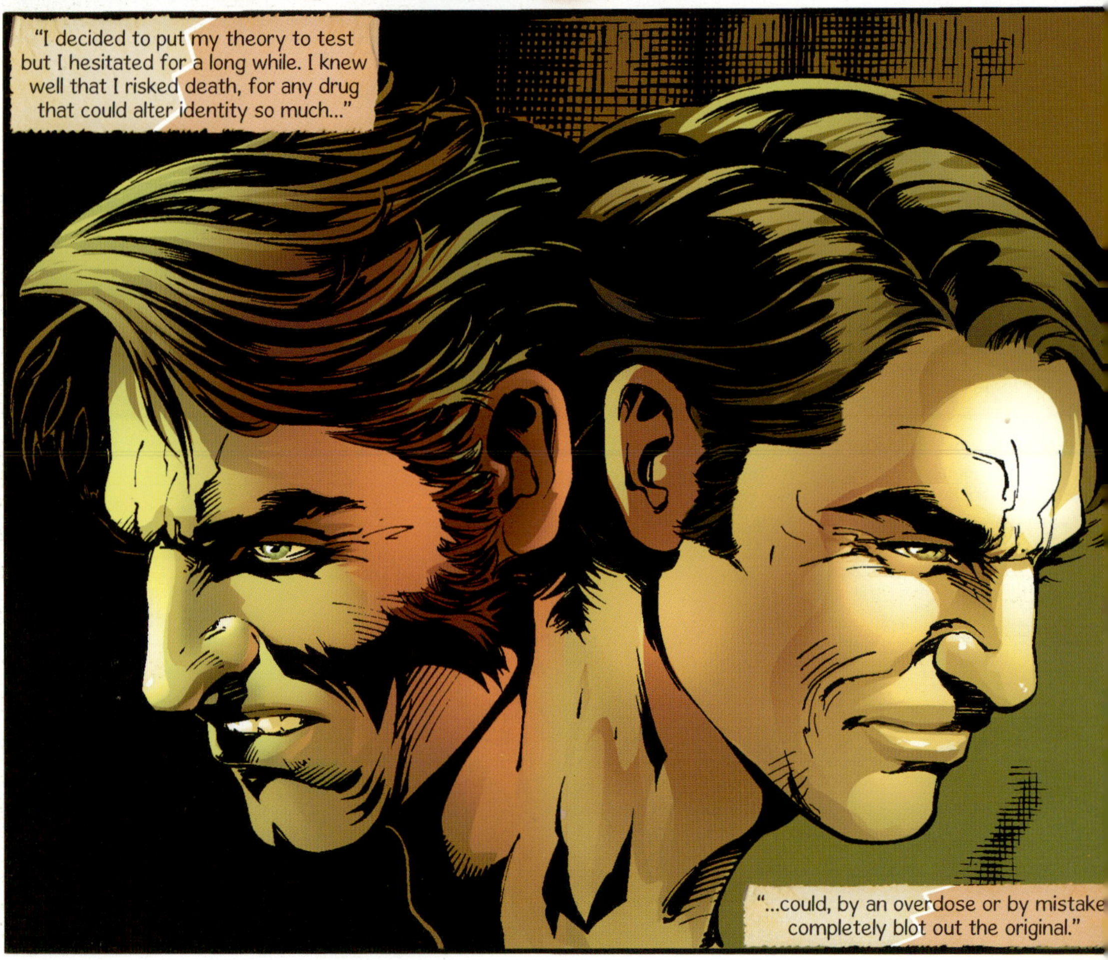
"I decided to put my theory to test but I hesitated for a long while. I knew well that I risked death, for any drug that could alter identity so much..."
"...could, by an overdose or by mistake completely blot out the original."

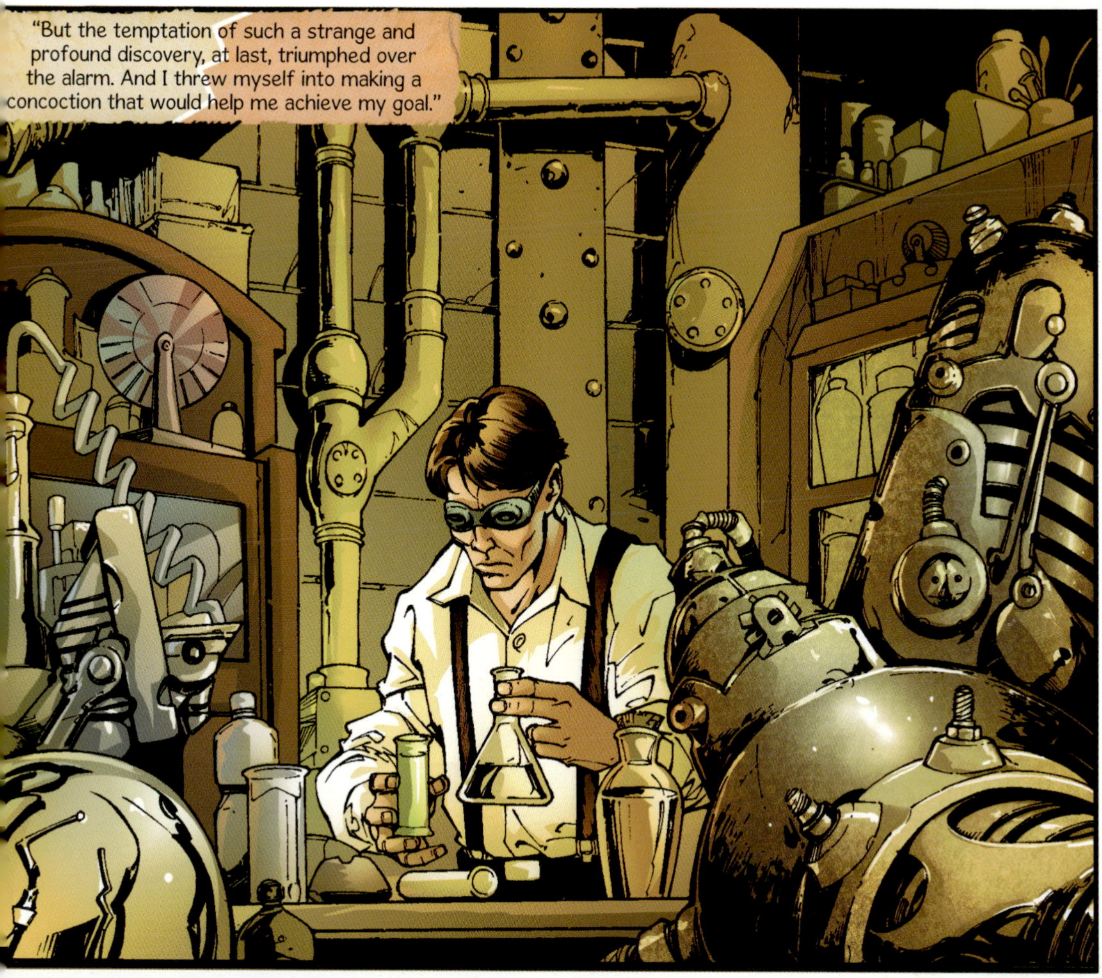
"But the temptation of such a strange and profound discovery, at last, triumphed over the alarm. And I threw myself into making a concoction that would help me achieve my goal."

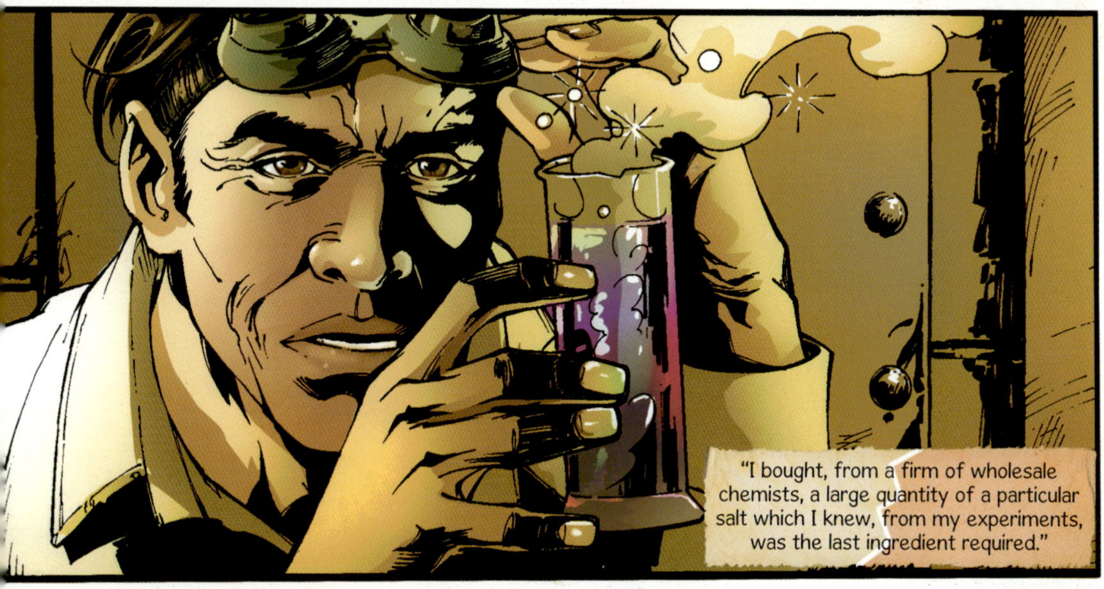
"I bought, from a firm of wholesale chemists, a large quantity of a particular salt which I knew, from my experiments, was the last ingredient required."

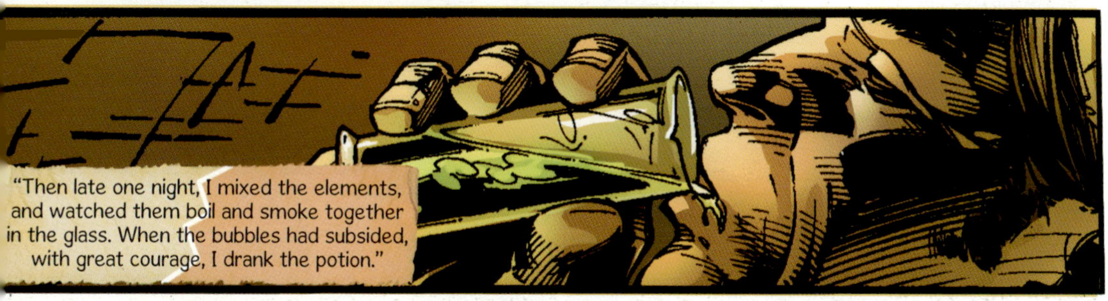
"Then late one night, I mixed the elements, and watched them boil and smoke together in the glass. When the bubbles had subsided, with great courage, I drank the potion."

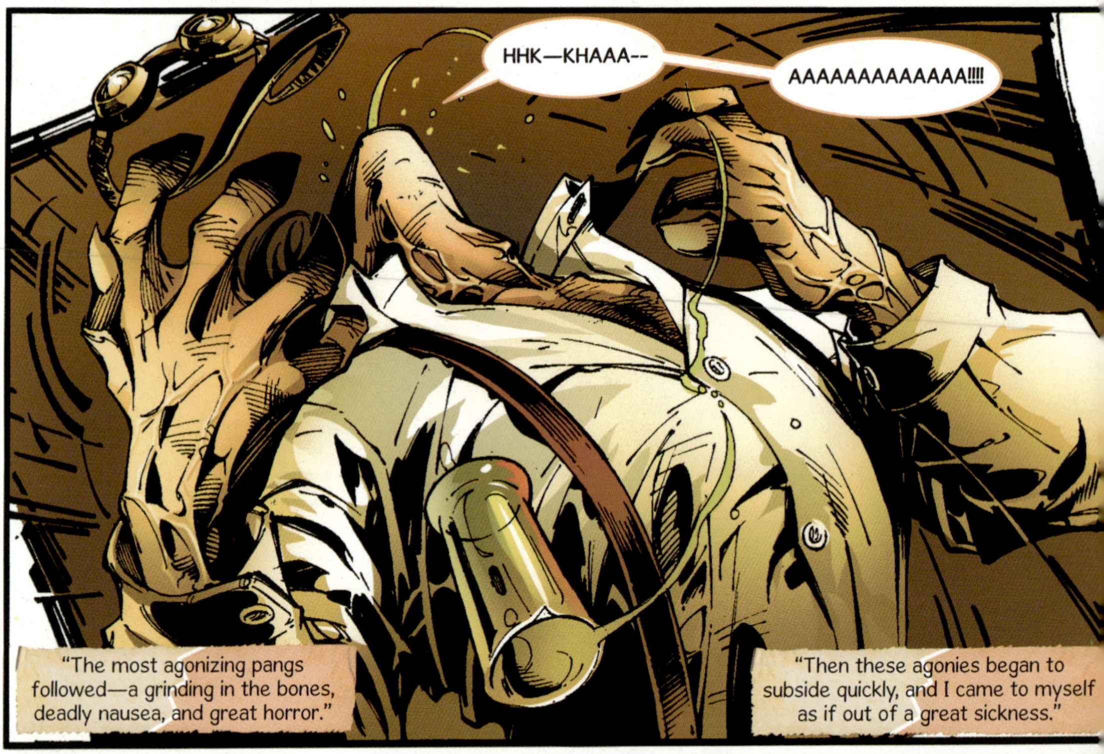
HHK—KHAAA--
AAAAAAAAAAAAA!!!!
"The most agonizing pangs followed—a grinding in the bones, deadly nausea, and great horror."
"Then these agonies began to subside quickly, and I came to myself as if out of a great sickness."
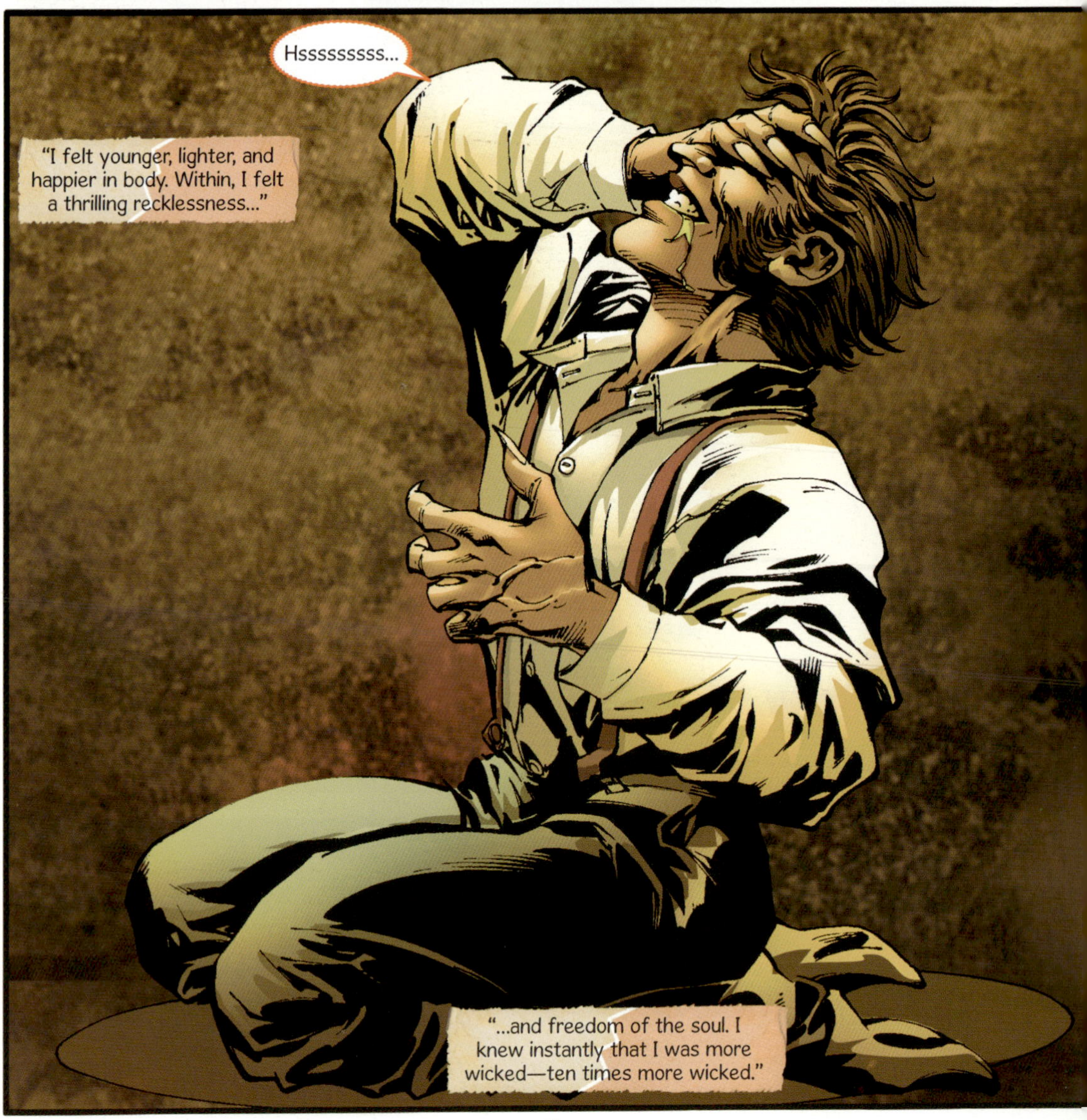
Hssssssss...
"I felt younger, lighter, and happier in body. Within, I felt a thrilling recklessness..."
"...and freedom of the soul. I knew instantly that I was more wicked—ten times more wicked."

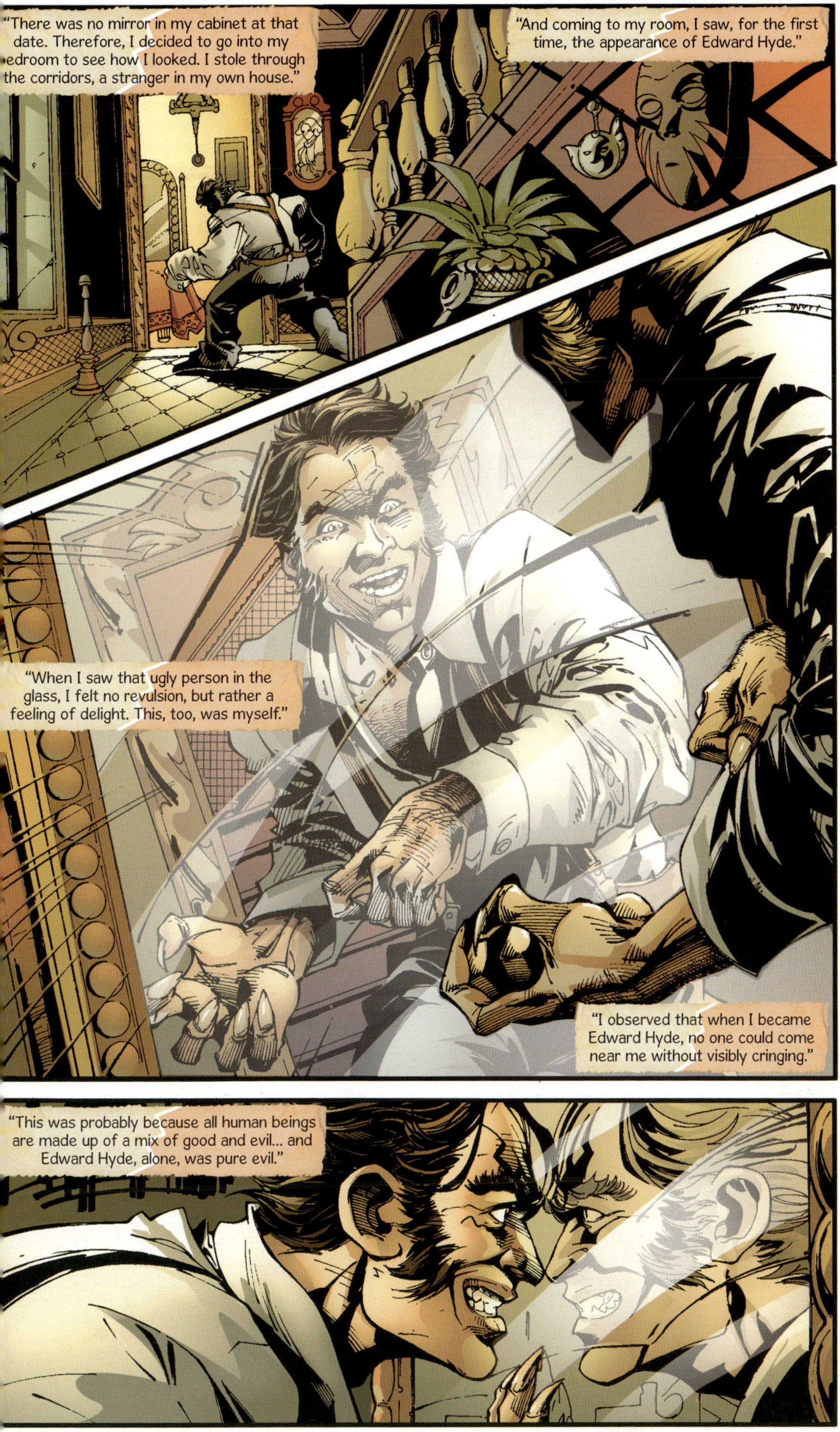
"There was no mirror in my cabinet at that date. Therefore, I decided to go into my bedroom to see how I looked. I stole through the corridors, a stranger in my own house."
"And coming to my room, I saw, for the first time, the appearance of Edward Hyde."
"When I saw that ugly person in the glass, I felt no revulsion, but rather a feeling of delight. This, too, was myself."
"I observed that when I became Edward Hyde, no one could come near me without visibly cringing."
"This was probably because all human beings are made up of a mix of good and evil... and Edward Hyde, alone, was pure evil."

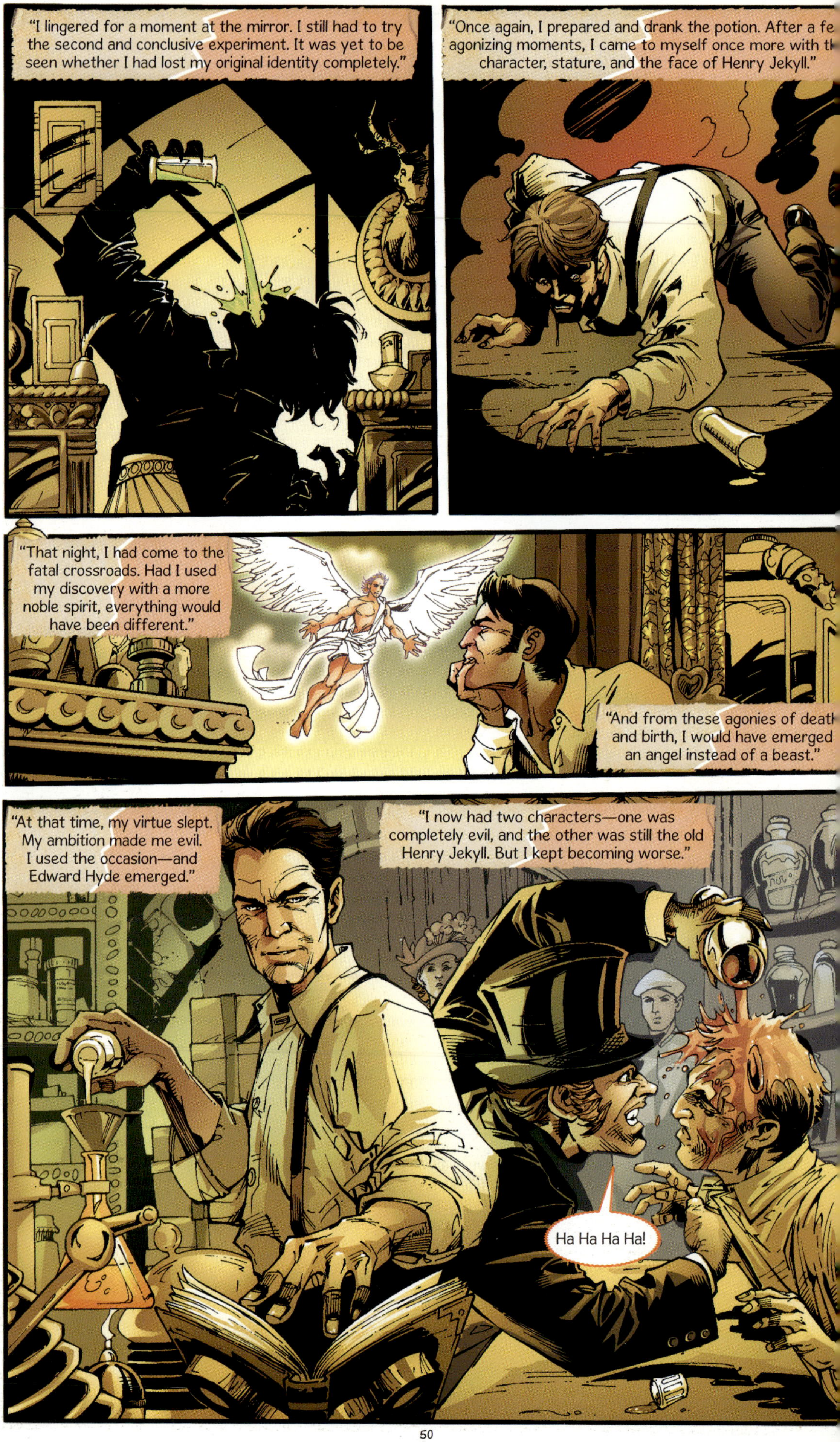
"I lingered for a moment at the mirror. I still had to try the second and conclusive experiment. It was yet to be seen whether I had lost my original identity completely."
"Once again, I prepared and drank the potion. After a fe agonizing moments, I came to myself once more with th character, stature, and the face of Henry Jekyll."
"That night, I had come to the fatal crossroads. Had I used my discovery with a more noble spirit, everything would have been different."
"And from these agonies of death and birth, I would have emerged an angel instead of a beast."
"At that time, my virtue slept. My ambition made me evil. I used the occasion—and Edward Hyde emerged."
"I now had two characters—one was completely evil, and the other was still the old Henry Jekyll. But I kept becoming worse."
Ha Ha Ha Ha!

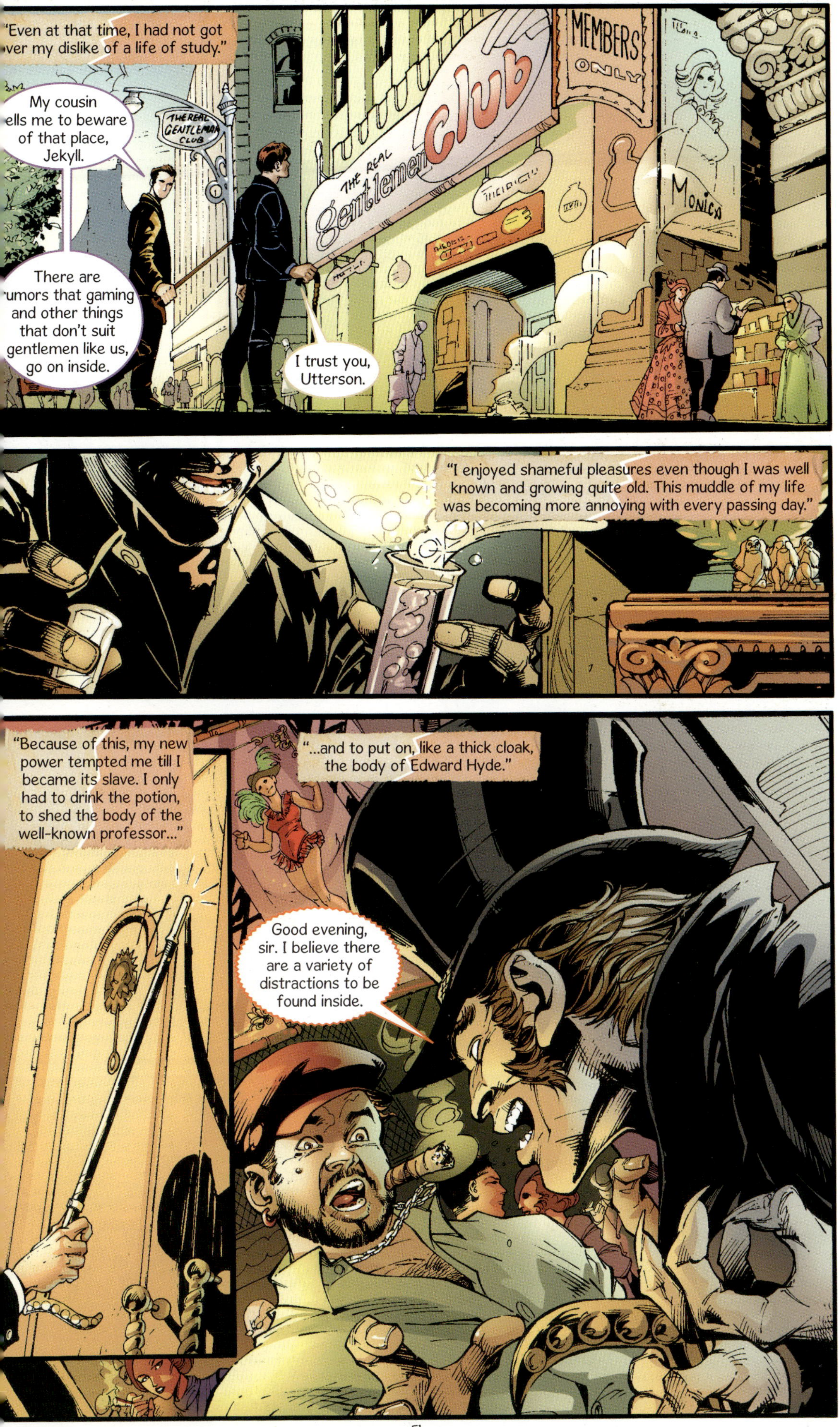
'Even at that time, I had not got
ver my dislike of a life of study."
My cousin
ells me to beware
of that place,
Jekyll.
There are
umors that gaming
and other things
that don't suit
gentlemen like us,
go on inside.
I trust you,
Utterson.
THE REAL GENTLEMAN CLUB
THE REAL gentlemen club
MEMBERS ONLY
Monica
"I enjoyed shameful pleasures even though I was well known and growing quite old. This muddle of my life was becoming more annoying with every passing day."
"Because of this, my new power tempted me till I became its slave. I only had to drink the potion, to shed the body of the well-known professor..."
"...and to put on, like a thick cloak, the body of Edward Hyde."
Good evening, sir. I believe there are a variety of distractions to be found inside.

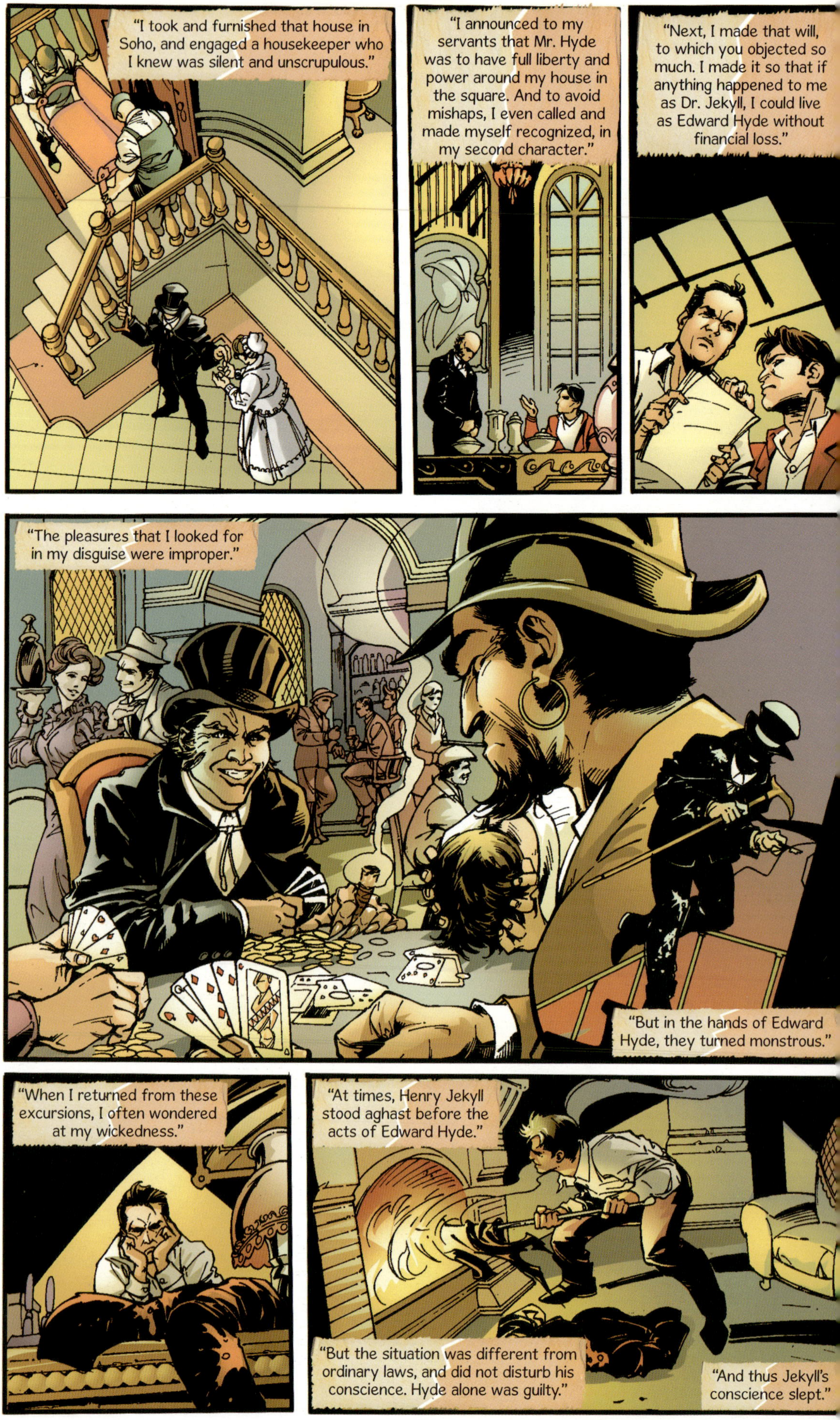
"I took and furnished that house in Soho, and engaged a housekeeper who I knew was silent and unscrupulous."
"I announced to my servants that Mr. Hyde was to have full liberty and power around my house in the square. And to avoid mishaps, I even called and made myself recognized, in my second character."
"Next, I made that will, to which you objected so much. I made it so that if anything happened to me as Dr. Jekyll, I could live as Edward Hyde without financial loss."
"The pleasures that I looked for in my disguise were improper."
"But in the hands of Edward Hyde, they turned monstrous."
"When I returned from these excursions, I often wondered at my wickedness."
"At times, Henry Jekyll stood aghast before the acts of Edward Hyde."
"But the situation was different from ordinary laws, and did not disturb his conscience. Hyde alone was guilty."
"And thus Jekyll's conscience slept."

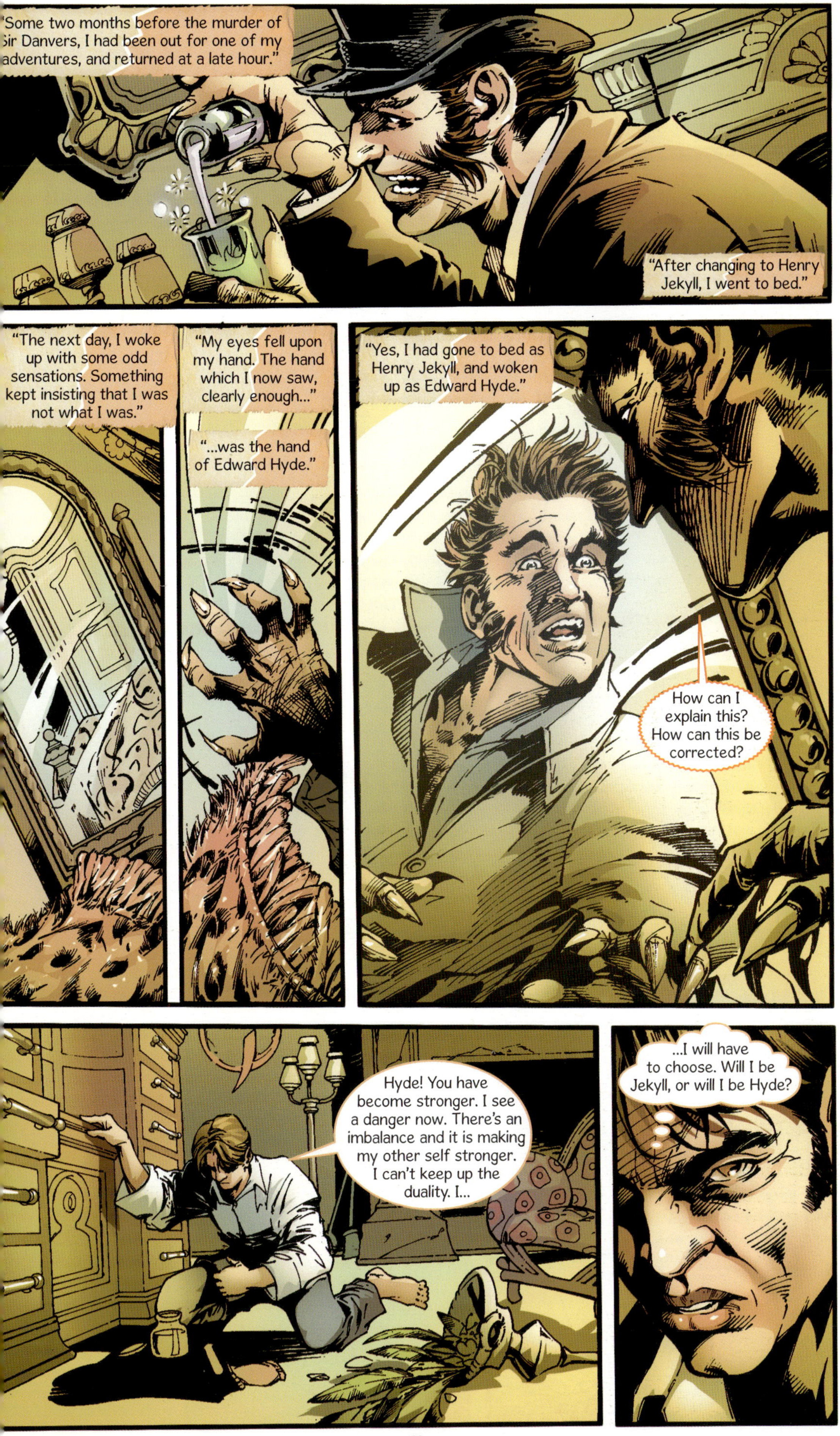
"Some two months before the murder of Sir Danvers, I had been out for one of my adventures, and returned at a late hour."
"After changing to Henry Jekyll, I went to bed."
"The next day, I woke up with some odd sensations. Something kept insisting that I was not what I was."
"My eyes fell upon my hand. The hand which I now saw, clearly enough..."
"...was the hand of Edward Hyde."
"Yes, I had gone to bed as Henry Jekyll, and woken up as Edward Hyde."
How can I explain this? How can this be corrected?
Hyde! You have become stronger. I see a danger now. There's an imbalance and it is making my other self stronger. I can't keep up the duality. I...
...I will have to choose. Will I be Jekyll, or will I be Hyde?

But how to choose? Jekyll, with a greedy gusto, shares the pleasures and adventures of Hyde.

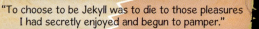

"To choose to be Jekyll was to die to those pleasures I had secretly enjoyed and begun to pamper."

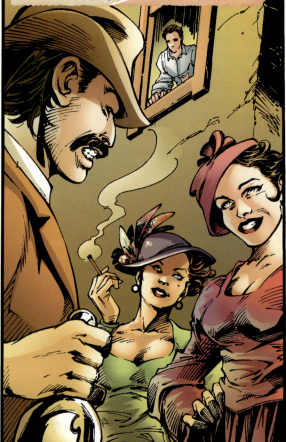

"To be Hyde was to die to a thousand interests and ambitions, and to become, forever, despised and friendless."

"And it happened with me—as it happens with most of my fellow men—that I chose the better part, but did not have the strength to stick to it."

"Yes, I chose to be the discontented doctor, surrounded by friends and cherishing honest hopes. And I bade a firm farewell to the secret pleasures I had enjoyed as Hyde."

"But I neither gave up the house in Soho, nor destroyed the clothes of Edward Hyde, which still remained in my cabinet."

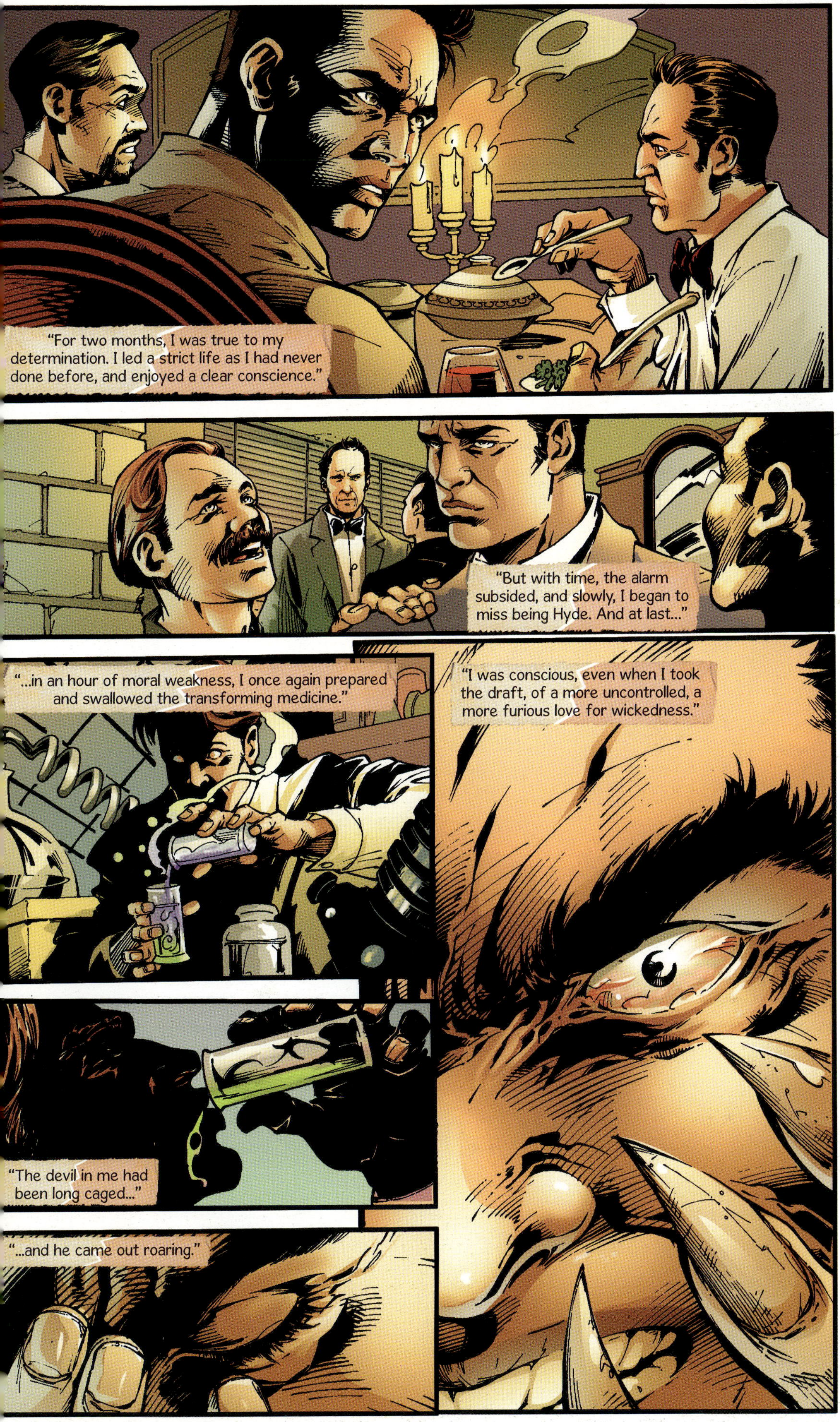
"For two months, I was true to my determination. I led a strict life as I had never done before, and enjoyed a clear conscience."
"But with time, the alarm subsided, and slowly, I began to miss being Hyde. And at last..."
"...in an hour of moral weakness, I once again prepared and swallowed the transforming medicine."
"I was conscious, even when I took the draft, of a more uncontrolled, a more furious love for wickedness."
"The devil in me had been long caged..."
"...and he came out roaring."

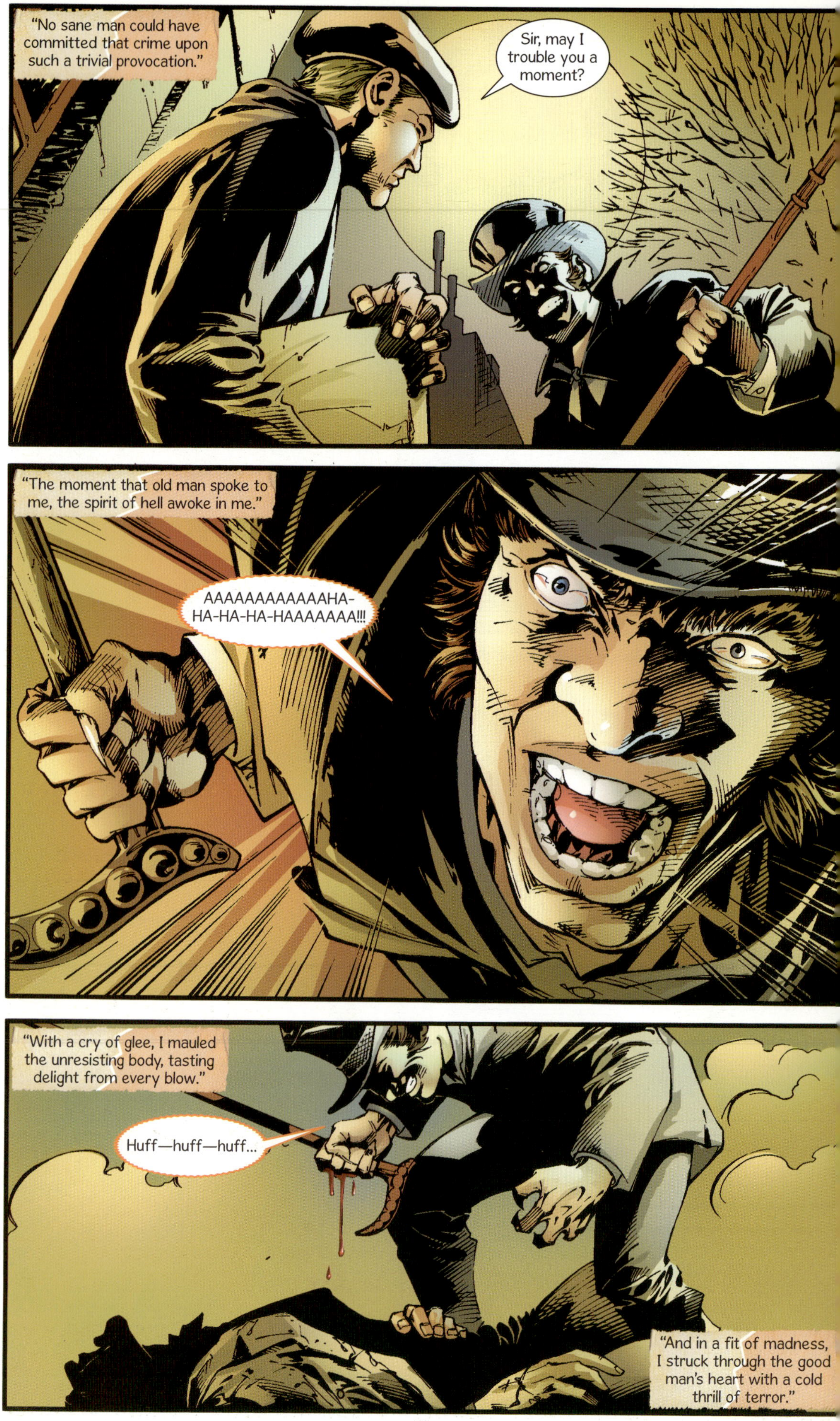
"No sane man could have committed that crime upon such a trivial provocation."
Sir, may I trouble you a moment?
"The moment that old man spoke to me, the spirit of hell awoke in me."
AAAAAAAAAAAAHA-HA-HA-HA-HAAAAAAA!!!
"With a cry of glee, I mauled the unresisting body, tasting delight from every blow."
Huff—huff—huff...
"And in a fit of madness, I struck through the good man's heart with a cold thrill of terror."

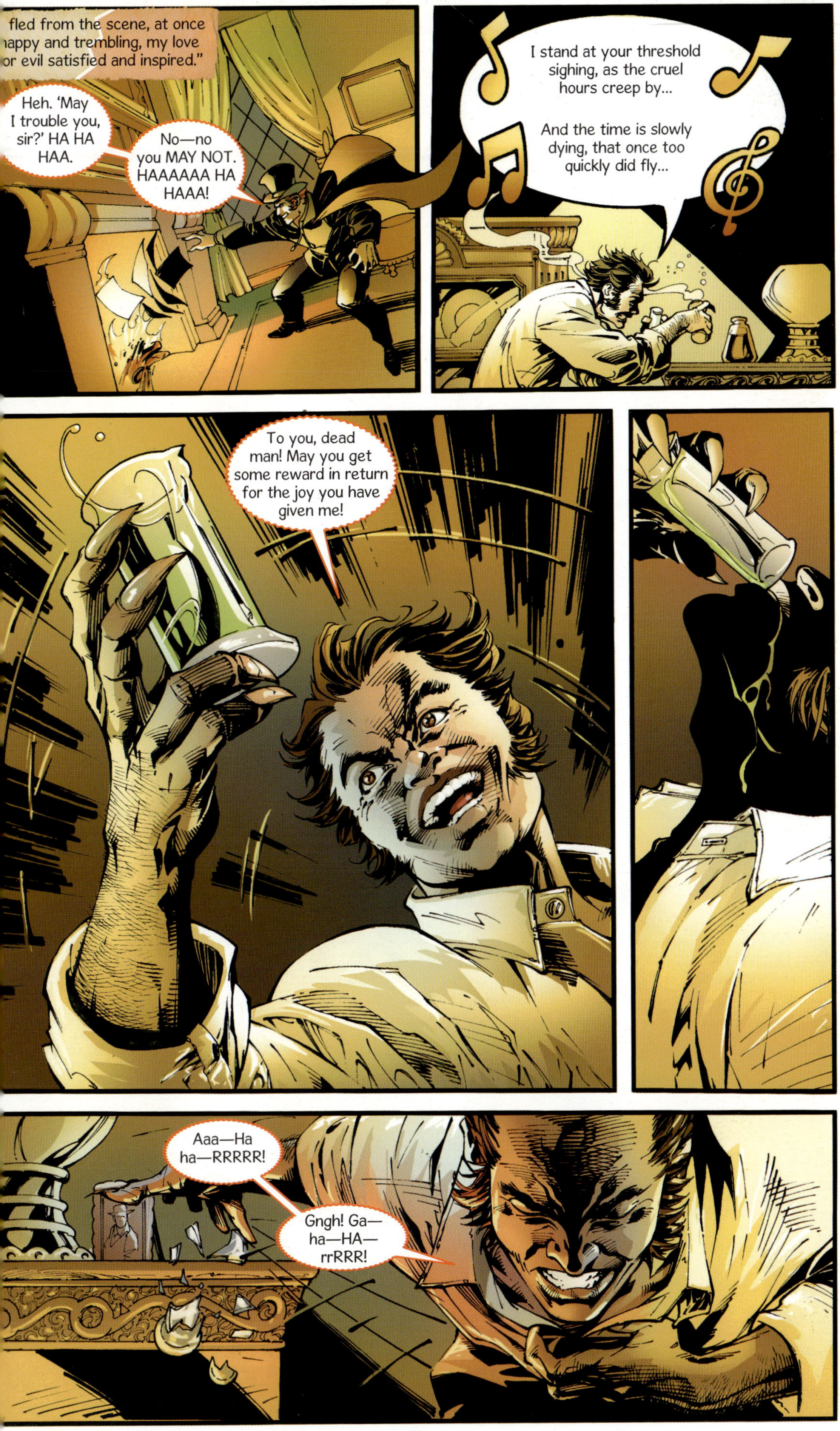
fled from the scene, at once
happy and trembling, my love
or evil satisfied and inspired."
Heh. 'May I trouble you, sir?' HA HA HAA.
No—no you MAY NOT. HAAAAAA HA HAAA!
I stand at your threshold sighing, as the cruel hours creep by...
And the time is slowly dying, that once too quickly did fly...
To you, dead man! May you get some reward in return for the joy you have given me!
Aaa—Ha ha—RRRRR!
Gngh! Ga—ha—HA—rrRRR!

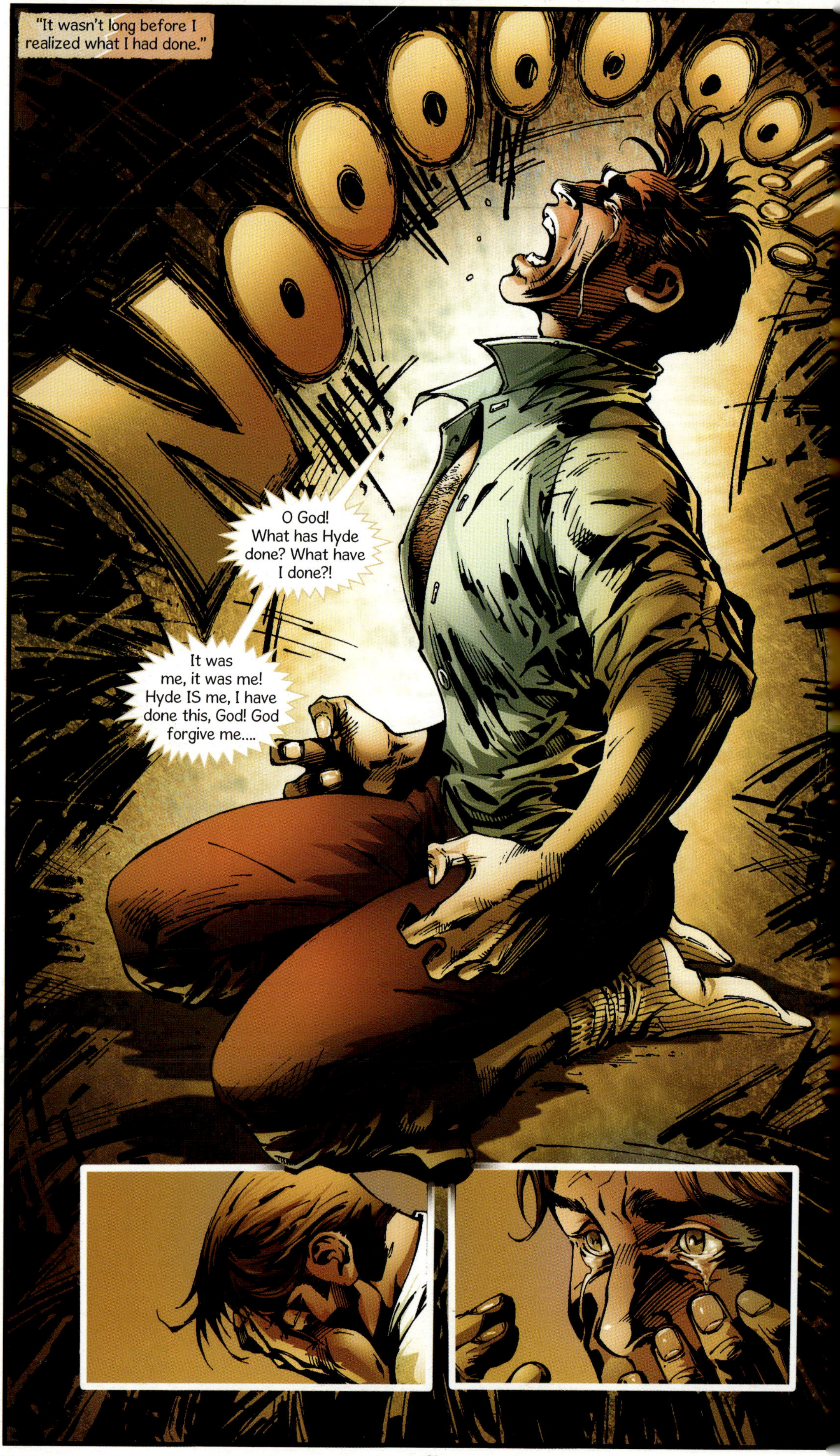
"It wasn't long before I realized what I had done."
NOOOOOOOOOOO
O God! What has Hyde done? What have I done?!
It was me, it was me! Hyde IS me, I have done this, God! God forgive me....

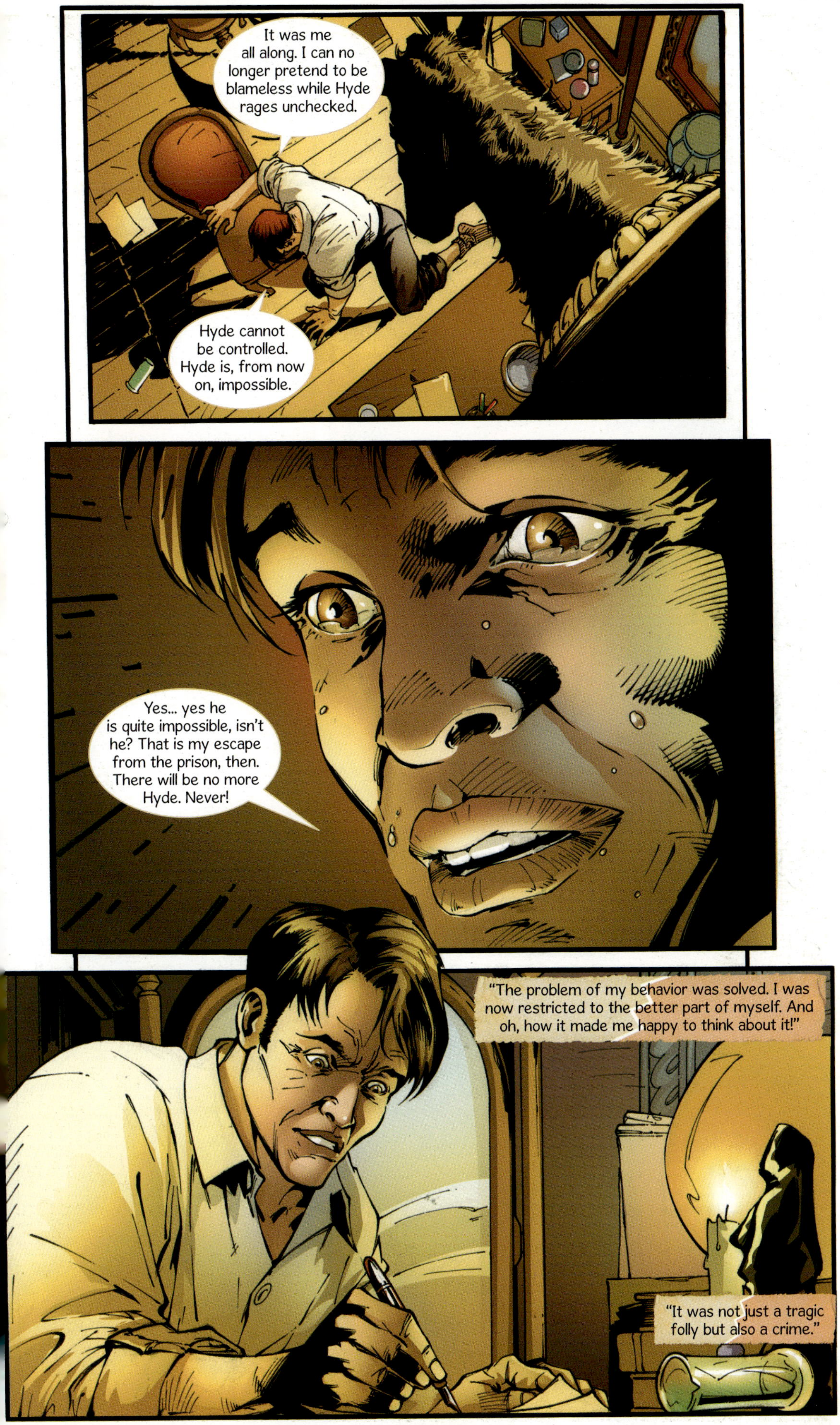
It was me all along. I can no longer pretend to be blameless while Hyde rages unchecked.
Hyde cannot be controlled. Hyde is, from now on, impossible.
Yes... yes he is quite impossible, isn't he? That is my escape from the prison, then. There will be no more Hyde. Never!
"The problem of my behavior was solved. I was now restricted to the better part of myself. And oh, how it made me happy to think about it!"
"It was not just a tragic folly but also a crime."

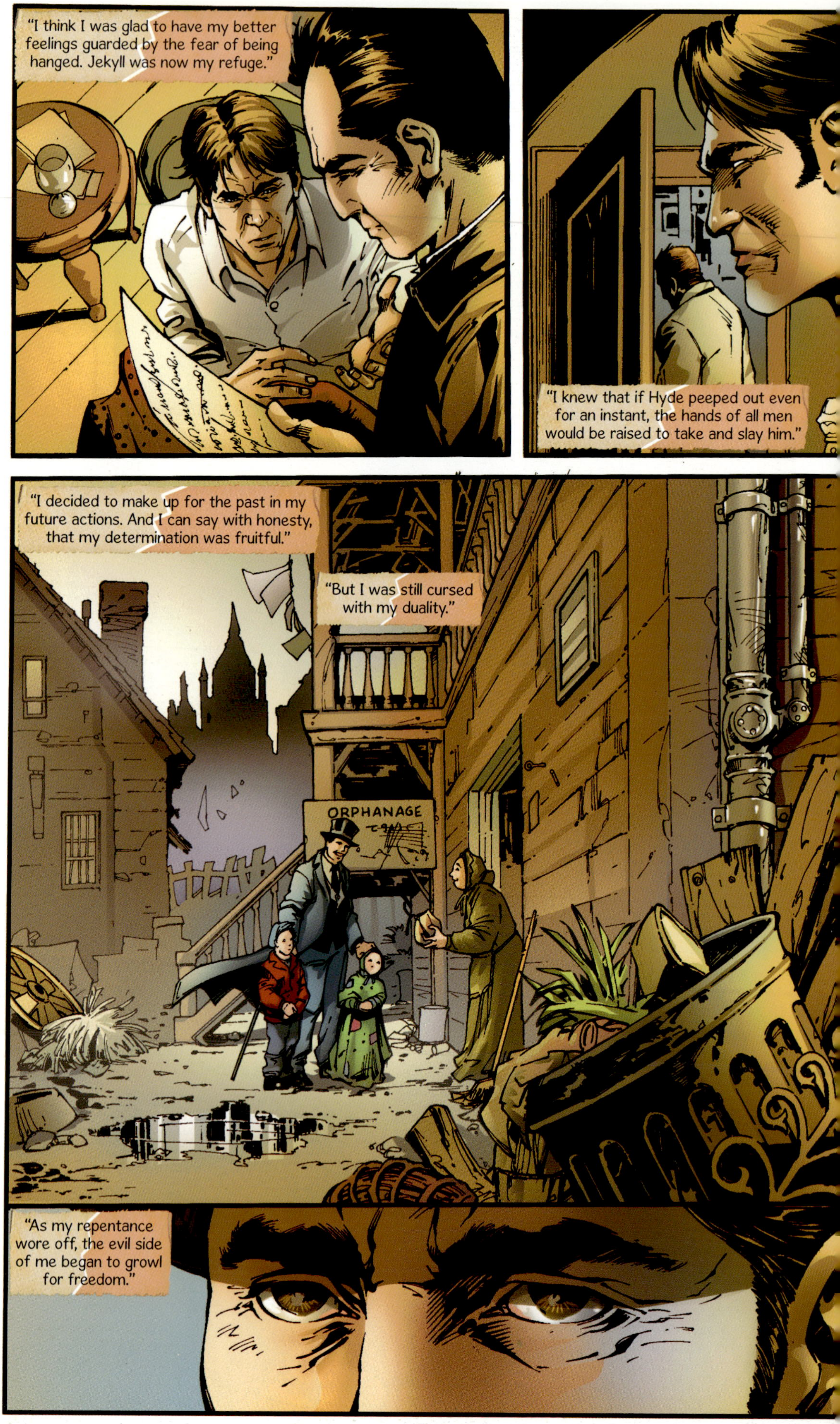
"I think I was glad to have my better feelings guarded by the fear of being hanged. Jekyll was now my refuge."
"I knew that if Hyde peeped out even for an instant, the hands of all men would be raised to take and slay him."
"I decided to make up for the past in my future actions. And I can say with honesty, that my determination was fruitful."
"But I was still cursed with my duality."
ORPHANAGE
"As my repentance wore off, the evil side of me began to growl for freedom."

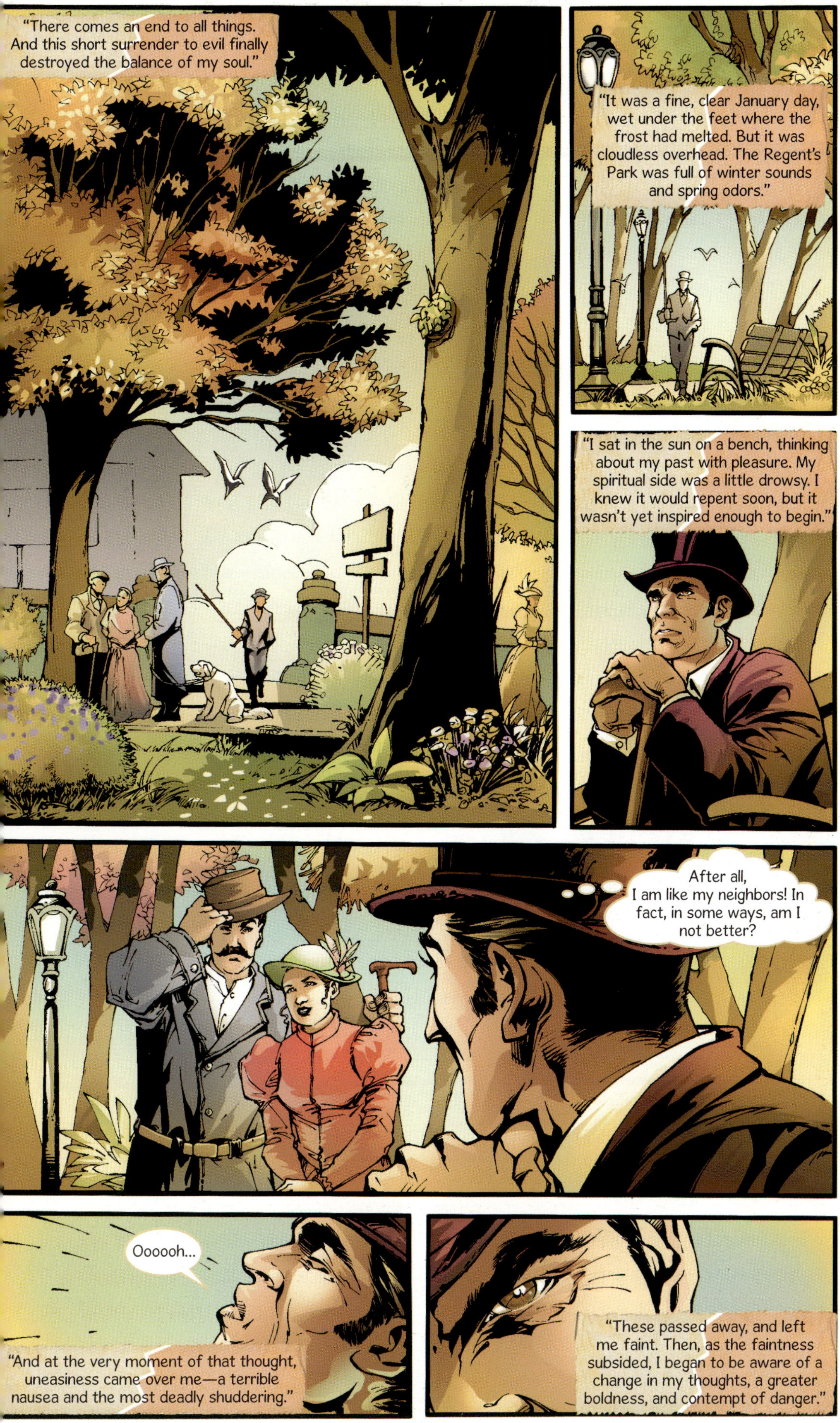
"There comes an end to all things. And this short surrender to evil finally destroyed the balance of my soul."
"It was a fine, clear January day, wet under the feet where the frost had melted. But it was cloudless overhead. The Regent's Park was full of winter sounds and spring odors."
"I sat in the sun on a bench, thinking about my past with pleasure. My spiritual side was a little drowsy. I knew it would repent soon, but it wasn't yet inspired enough to begin."
After all, I am like my neighbors! In fact, in some ways, am I not better?
Oooooh...
"And at the very moment of that thought, uneasiness came over me—a terrible nausea and the most deadly shuddering."
"These passed away, and left me faint. Then, as the faintness subsided, I began to be aware of a change in my thoughts, a greater boldness, and contempt of danger."

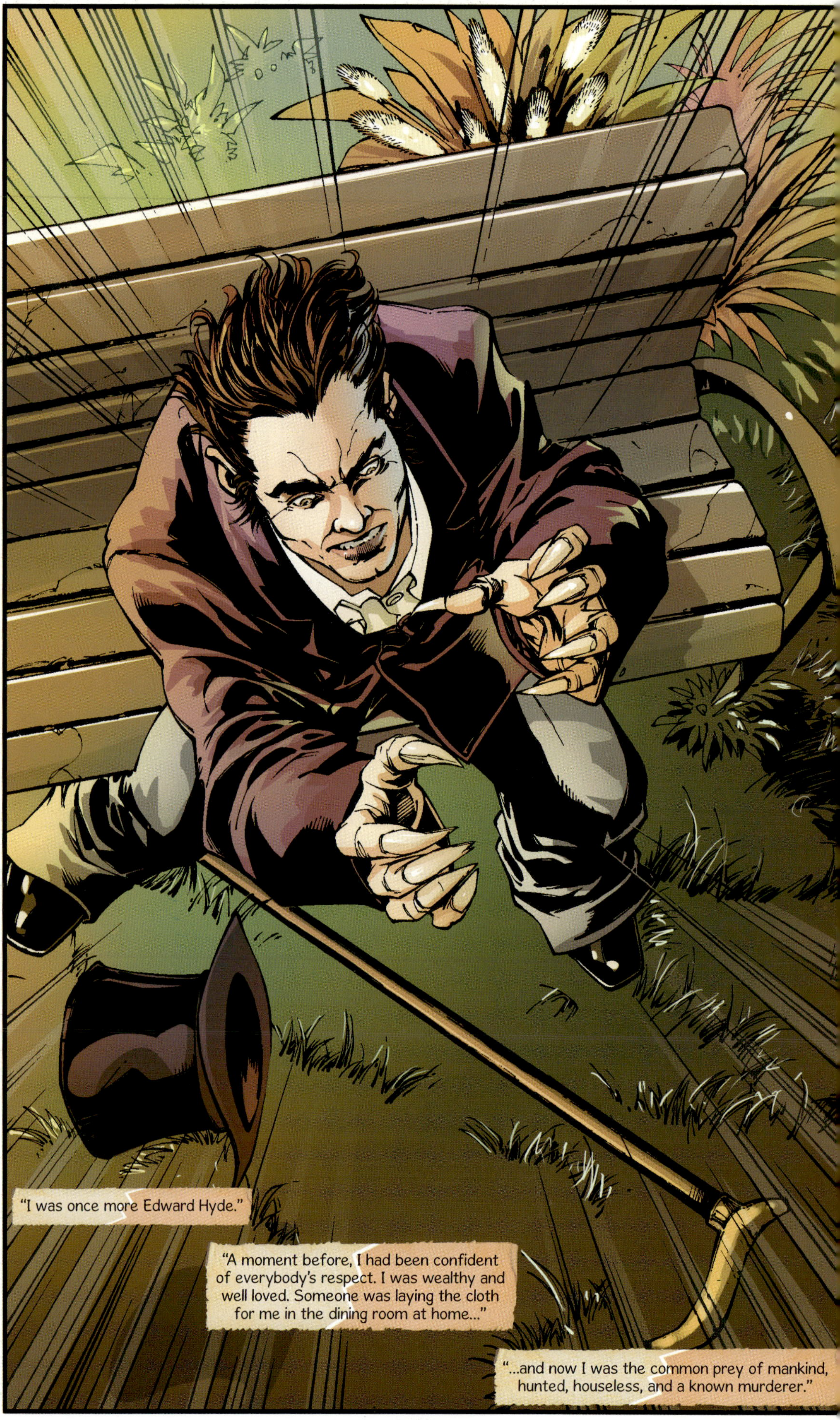
"I was once more Edward Hyde."
"A moment before, I had been confident of everybody's respect. I was wealthy and well loved. Someone was laying the cloth for me in the dining room at home..."
"...and now I was the common prey of mankind, hunted, houseless, and a known murderer."

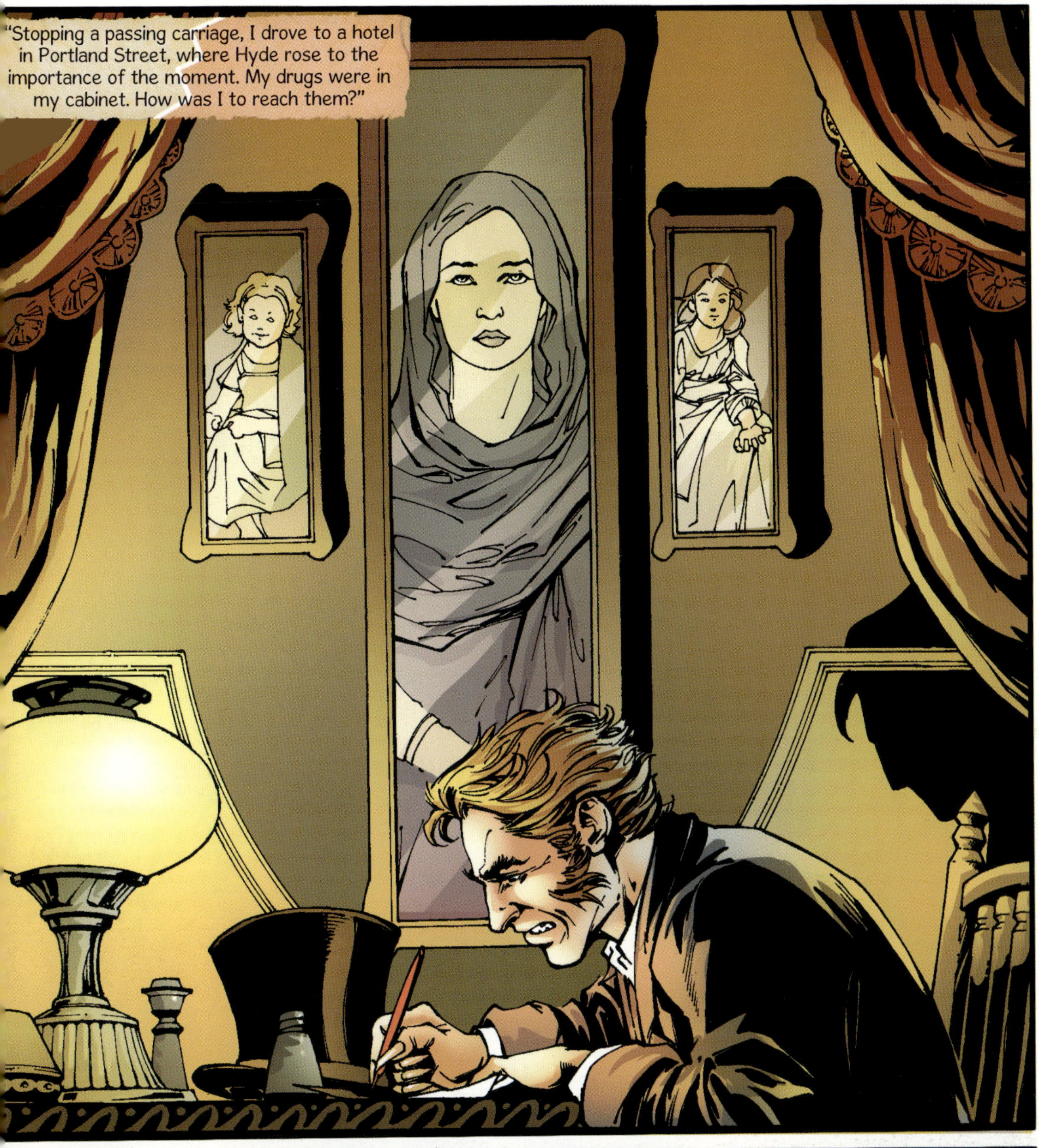
"Stopping a passing carriage, I drove to a hotel in Portland Street, where Hyde rose to the importance of the moment. My drugs were in my cabinet. How was I to reach them?"

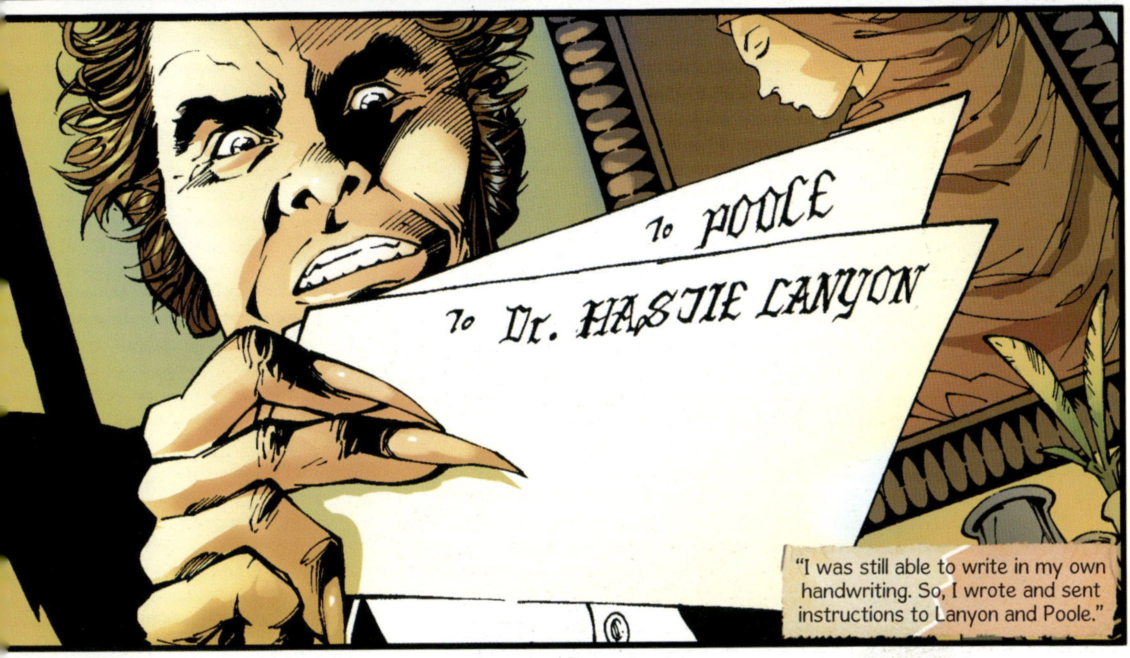
To POOLE
To Dr. HASTIE LANYON
"I was still able to write in my own handwriting. So, I wrote and sent instructions to Lanyon and Poole."

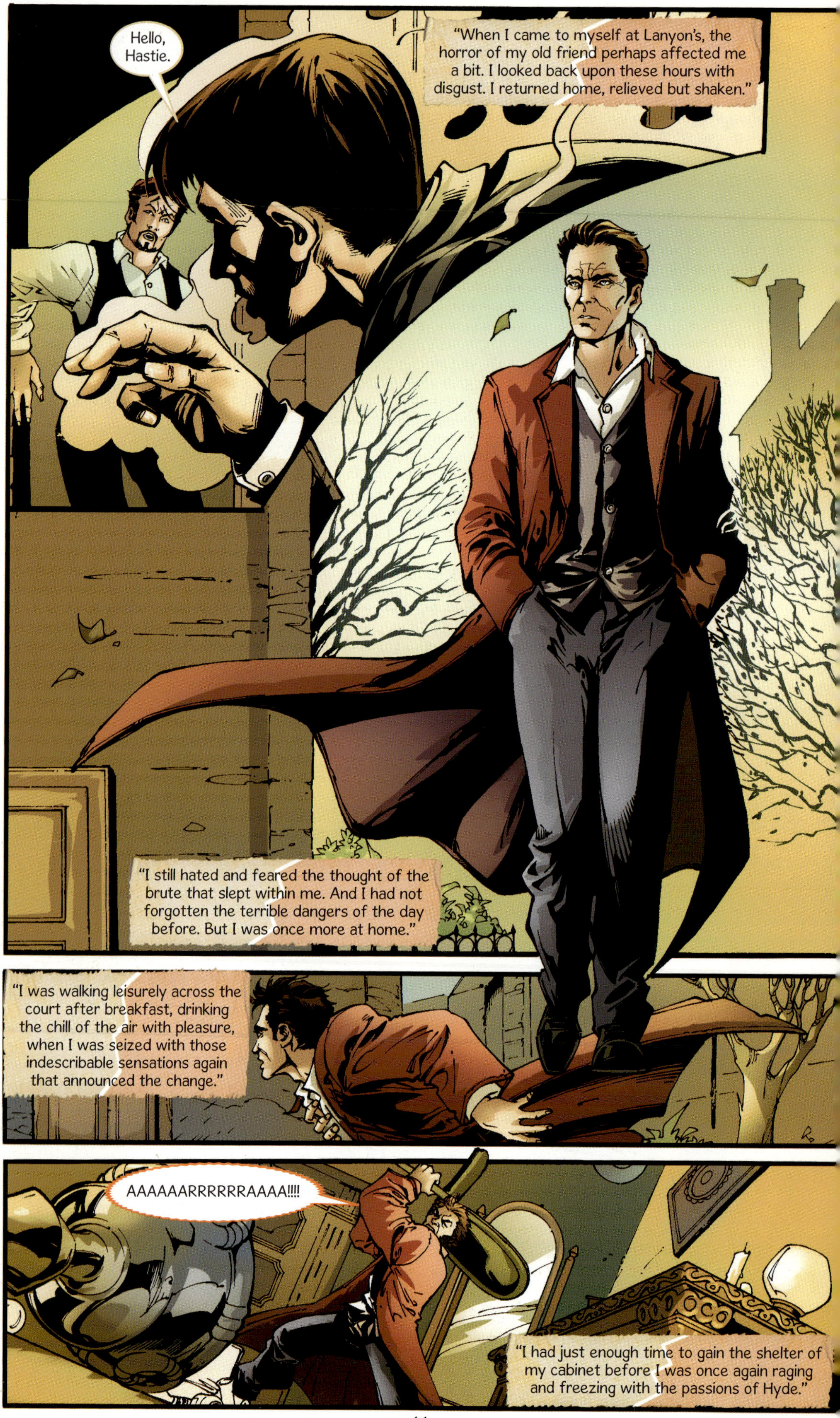
Hello, Hastie.
"When I came to myself at Lanyon's, the horror of my old friend perhaps affected me a bit. I looked back upon these hours with disgust. I returned home, relieved but shaken."
"I still hated and feared the thought of the brute that slept within me. And I had not forgotten the terrible dangers of the day before. But I was once more at home."
"I was walking leisurely across the court after breakfast, drinking the chill of the air with pleasure, when I was seized with those indescribable sensations again that announced the change."
AAAAAARRRRRRAAAA!!!!
"I had just enough time to gain the shelter of my cabinet before I was once again raging and freezing with the passions of Hyde."

"It took a double dose to bring me back to myself! From that day, only by great effort, and only under the influence of the drug, was I able to become Jekyll."

"At all hours of the day and night, I would shudder; and above all, if I slept, or even dozed for a moment in my chair..."

"...it was always as Hyde that I woke up."

"My provision of the salt, which had never been renewed since the first experiment, began to run low."

"I sent out for a fresh supply, and mixed the draft—the bubbles followed, and the first change of color happened..."

"...but not the second. I drank it and it was ineffective."

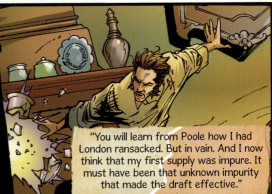

"You will learn from Poole how I had London ransacked. But in vain. And I now think that my first supply was impure. It must have been that unknown impurity that made the draft effective."

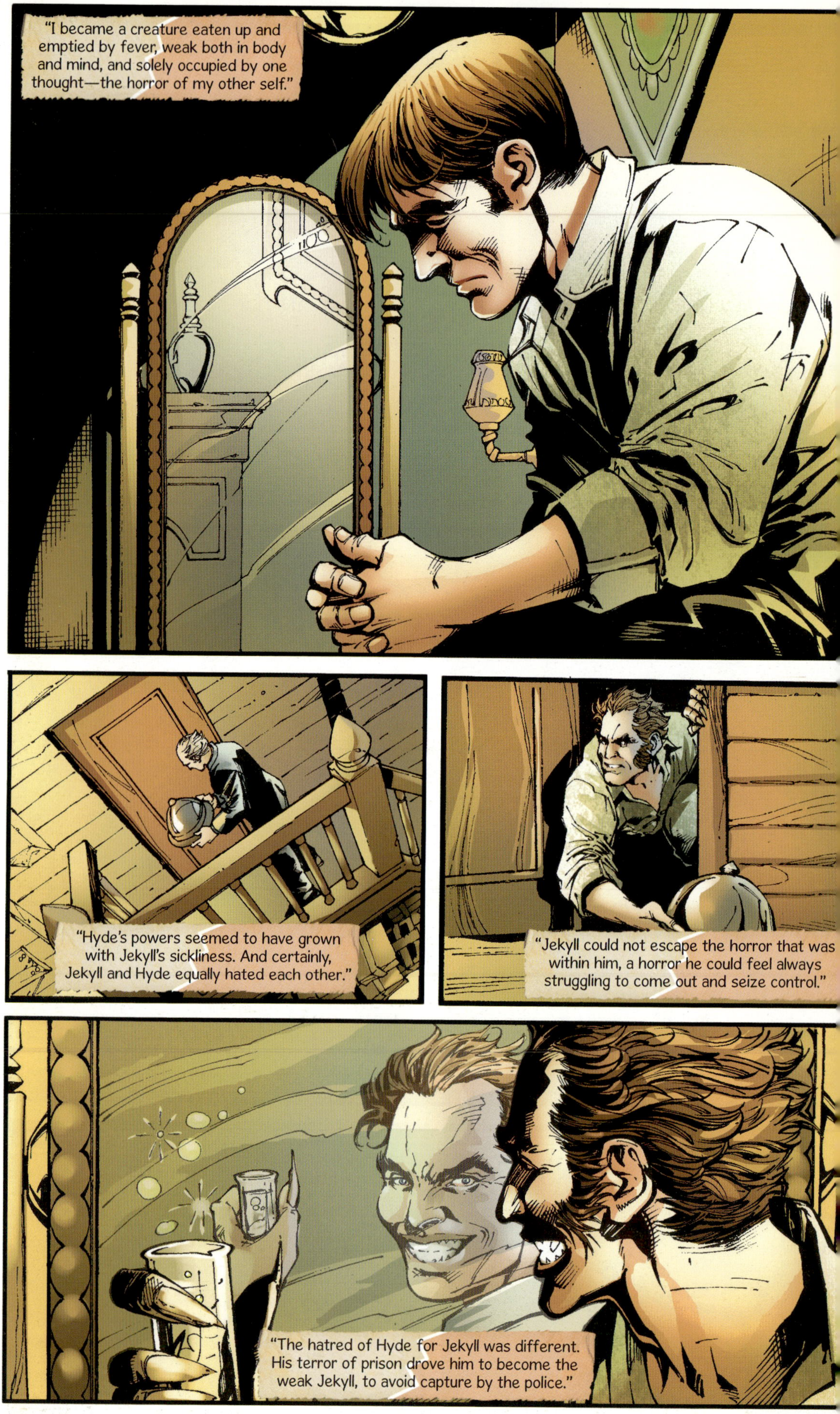
"I became a creature eaten up and emptied by fever, weak both in body and mind, and solely occupied by one thought—the horror of my other self."
"Hyde's powers seemed to have grown with Jekyll's sickliness. And certainly, Jekyll and Hyde equally hated each other."
"Jekyll could not escape the horror that was within him, a horror he could feel always struggling to come out and seize control."
"The hatred of Hyde for Jekyll was different. His terror of prison drove him to become the weak Jekyll, to avoid capture by the police."

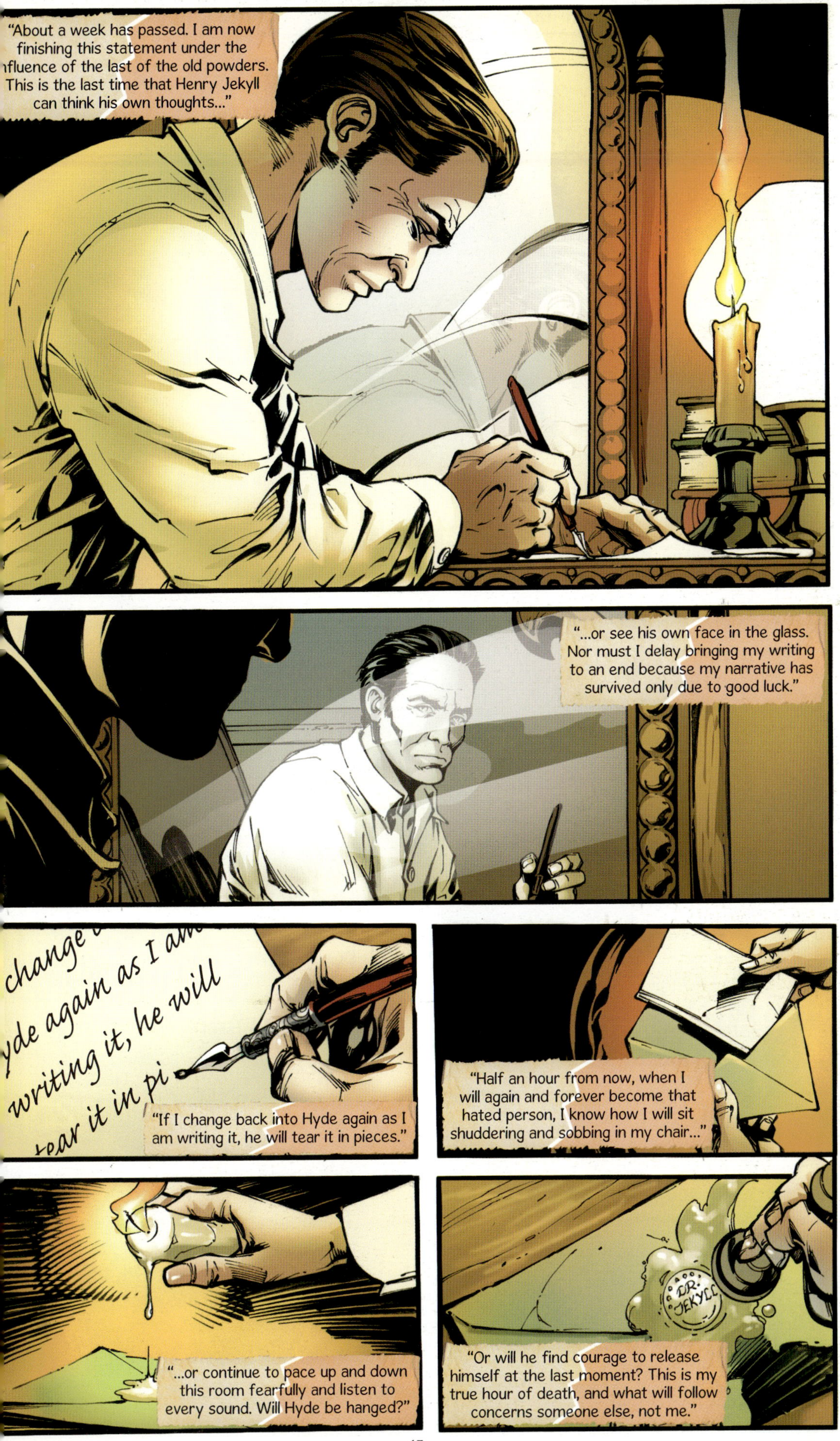
"About a week has passed. I am now finishing this statement under the nfluence of the last of the old powders. This is the last time that Henry Jekyll can think his own thoughts..."
"...or see his own face in the glass. Nor must I delay bringing my writing to an end because my narrative has survived only due to good luck."
change
yde again as I am
writing it, he will
tear it in pi
"If I change back into Hyde again as I am writing it, he will tear it in pieces."
"Half an hour from now, when I will again and forever become that hated person, I know how I will sit shuddering and sobbing in my chair..."
"...or continue to pace up and down this room fearfully and listen to every sound. Will Hyde be hanged?"
DR. JEKYLL
"Or will he find courage to release himself at the last moment? This is my true hour of death, and what will follow concerns someone else, not me."

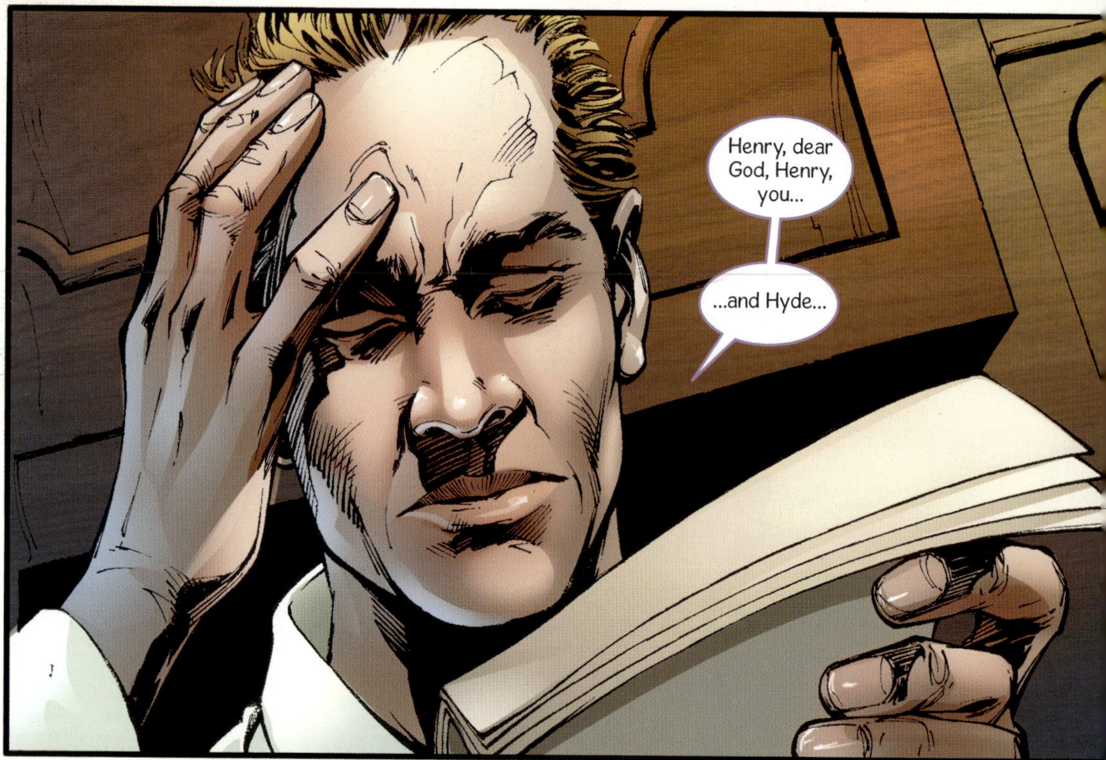
Henry, dear God, Henry, you...
...and Hyde...

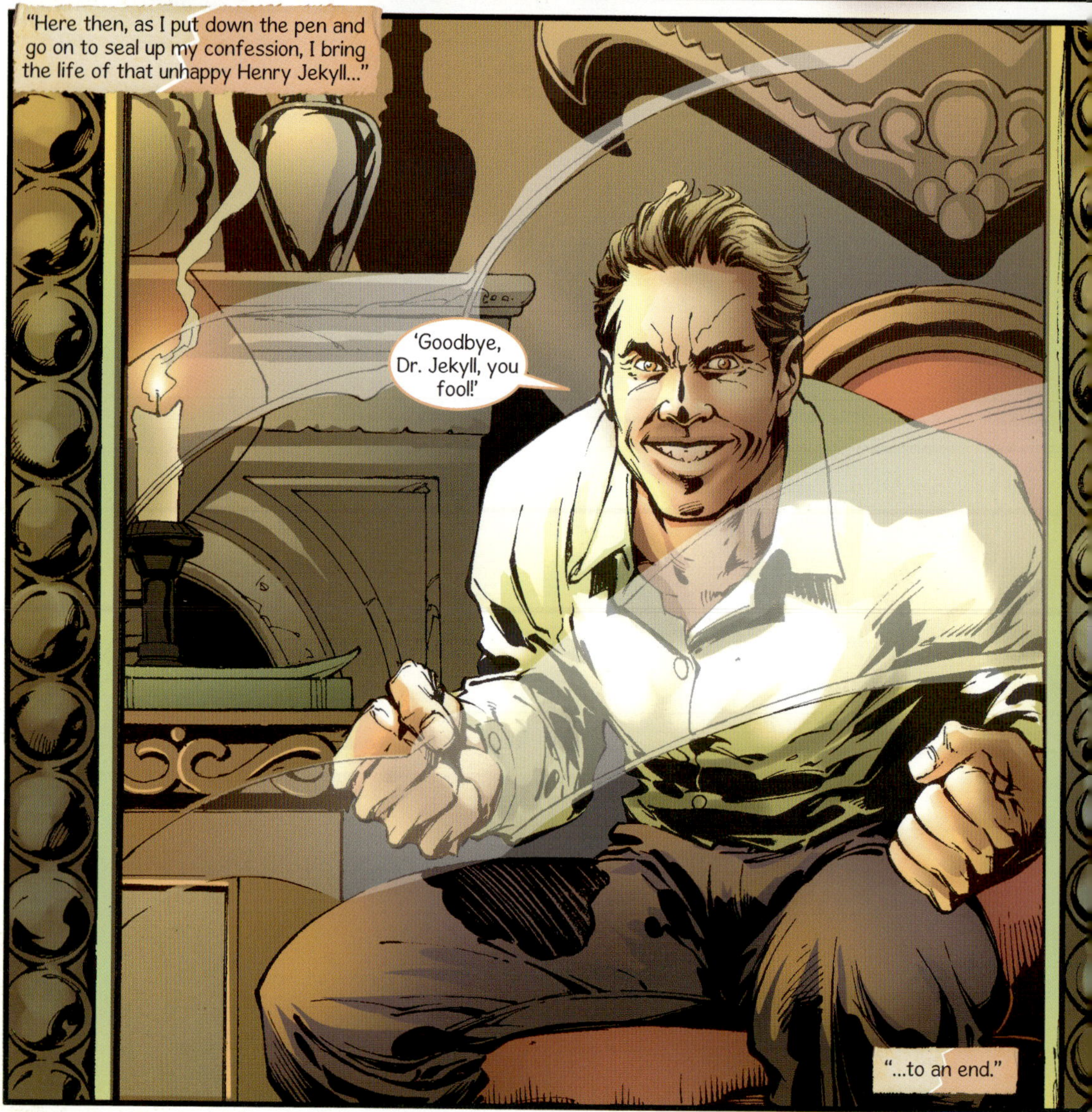
"Here then, as I put down the pen and go on to seal up my confession, I bring the life of that unhappy Henry Jekyll..."
'Goodbye, Dr. Jekyll, you fool!'
"...to an end."

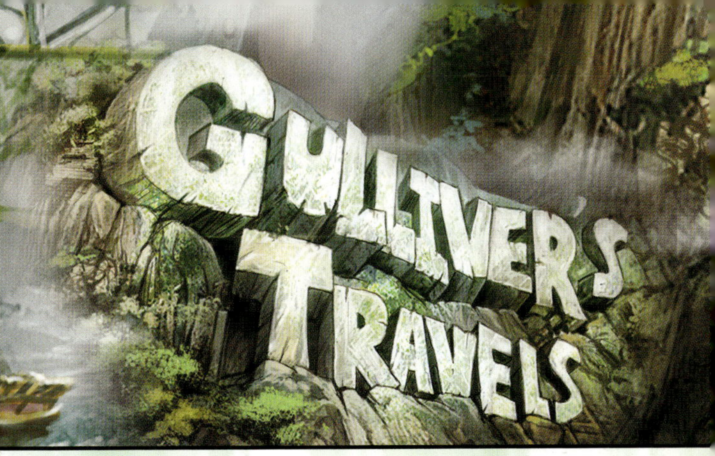
GULLIVER'S TRAVELS

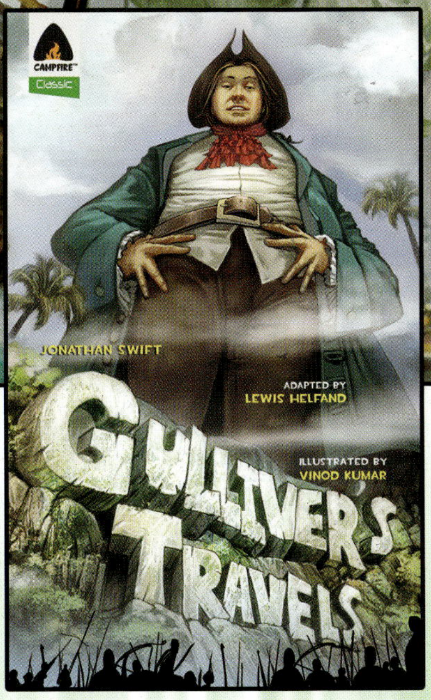
CAMPFIRE
Classic
JONATHAN SWIFT
ADAPTED BY
LEWIS HELFAND
ILLUSTRATED BY
VINOD KUMAR
GULLIVER'S TRAVELS

ADAPTED BY
LEWIS HELFAND

ILLUSTRATED BY
VINOD KUMAR

Travel to the exotic lands of giants, lilliputs, and hop on-board a flying island through the captivating accounts of a seventeenth-century explorer.

Lemuel Gulliver always dreamed of traveling the world. But when a violent storm claims his ship and casts him adrift among uncharted lands, he is taken to places that he could not even dream of.

Traveling to the nation of Lilliput, where the inhabitants measure just centimeters tall, and to Brobdingnag, where they tower into the sky like giants, Gulliver voyages to an island floating above the clouds, visits a race of immortals, and finds himself stranded in a land rule by horses.

Face to face with warring armies and power-hungry kings, each new journey makes Gulliver more desperate to find a way back home. But once he discovers the truth about his own land and himself… returning home becomes the last thing he desires.

Written by world-renowned satirist, Jonathan Swift, *Gulliver's Travels* is one of the most gripping and poignant adventures ever told.

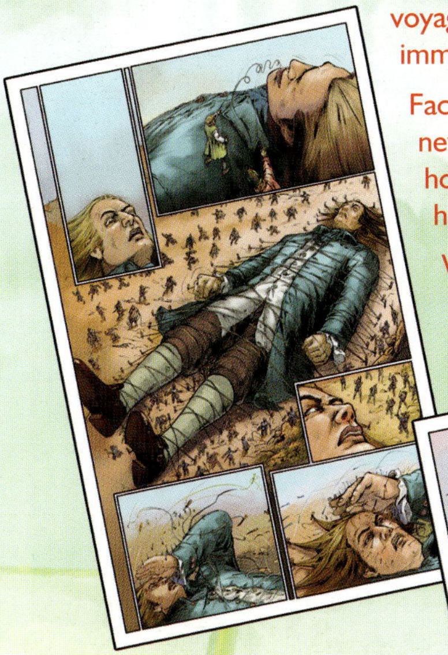

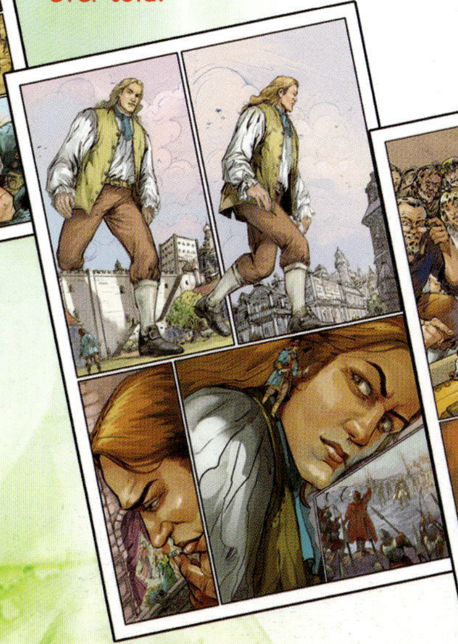

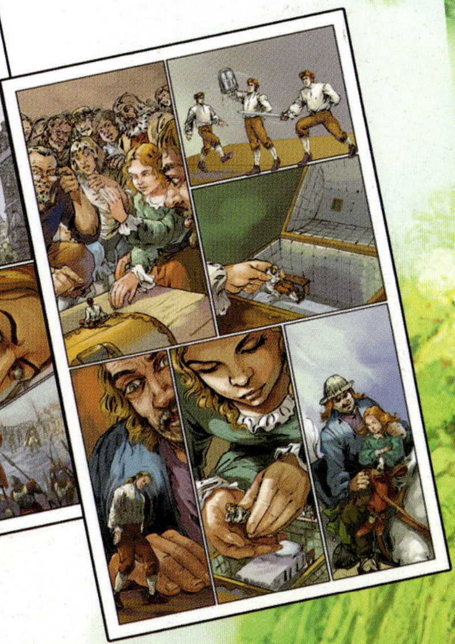

CAMPFIRE™
www.campfire.co.in

MAD SCIENTISTS

What comes to your mind when you hear the word scientist—someone dedicated to creating something new out of nothing or inventing new ideas or discovering some deep-rooted facts! But have you ever thought that while doing all these they can go to an extent where they can simply be termed as 'mad'! Read on to know about some mad scientists...

Giovanni Aldini

A 19th-century Italian physicist, Aldini worked with galvanism—electricity. He became famous, or rather infamous, for his horror shows! He went across Europe electrifying human and animal bodies in public. But it was his show at the Royal College of Surgeons in London in 1803 that earned him the title of 'mad scientist.' Aldini electrified the body of a hanged convict, George Forster, in this show. He attached conducting rods to the dead body whereby the body began to punch and kick his legs in the air. Rods on the face made it twitch. The left eye even flew open! People were frightened out of their wits. One person was so horrified that he reportedly died after the spectacle!

A 20th-century Russian biologist in the Stalinist era, Ivanov did really strange experiments on animals. He created hybrids like zedonks (zebra and donkey), an antelope-cow, a mouse-guinea pig, and a guinea pig-rabbit! But then, Ivanov deviated from this rather interesting track with his human-ape cross experiments! He attempted to create creatures which would be half-man and half-ape. Apparently, Stalin wanted to create an army of man-apes that would be unbeatable and insensitive to pain, and Ivanov was to help create one! Though he experimented with the idea, he did not really succeed as the whole idea was not taken kindly to!

Ilya Ivanovich Ivanov

Harry Harlow

A 20th-century psychologist, Harry Harlow contributed to the budding animal rights movement because of his cruelty to helpless animals. Harlow's most infamous experiments were conducted with rhesus monkeys. Wanting to study the mother-infant bonding, he separated infants from their mothers and offered them a choice of surrogate mothers—a wire mesh figure or a terrycloth covered figure, one provided milk and one did not. The names he gave to his various apparatuses, such as 'iron maiden' and 'pit of despair', gives an idea of how traumatized the poor baby monkeys must have been!

A 19th-century geologist and paleontologist, Buckland earned a place in the list of 'mad scientists' because he literally ate his way through the animal kingdom. He apparently ate all kinds of animals and insects, finding only moles and bluebottle flies inedible! If this was not enough, while on a visit to a museum, the preserved heart of a French king caught his attention. He decided he wanted to taste it, and, before anyone could stop him, he gobbled it up! That particular heart is said to have been that of Louis XIV. Buckland is believed to have gone 'officially' mad, and later ended up in an asylum!

Rev. William Buckland

Henry Cavendish

An 18th-century scientist, Cavendish isolated hydrogen to discover the famed H_2O formula and the density of the Earth. He was an introvert and a shy man—to the point of mania! He refused to have any direct contact with another human being. Even his housekeeper had to communicate with him through letters. But this level of isolation had drawbacks: other scientists were credited with laws and discoveries 150 years after he had found them! And since all his experiments were conducted alone, he himself had to be the test subject and had to conduct experiments, including self-electrocution!

A 20th-century Soviet scientist and organ transplant pioneer, Demikhov did several transplantations in the 1930s and 1950s. The transplantation of a heart into an animal and a lung-heart replacement were among them. But he became infamous for his strange experiments on dogs! He tried to create a two-headed dog in a most bizarre manner. This unfortunate beast had been created by attaching the head and upper body of a small puppy on the head and body of a fully-grown dog, to form one grotesque creature with two heads!

Vladimir Demikhov